Praise for Christopher Wilkins's
The Horizontal Instrument

'The most compelling novella I have read in decades . . .
Christopher Wilkins has broadened my sympathies and
understanding of human predicaments. The book is sparely
and beautifully written'
Alec Guinness, *Sunday Telegraph (Books of the Year)*

'Marvellous . . . by writing with calm, careful precision
about time, memory and love, Christopher Wilkins has
written an extraordinarily moving novel about everything
that matters'
Patrick Skene Catling, *Spectator*

'An intriguing meditation on time . . . In yielding to
the imperative of emotion, and acknowledging loss and
grief over the perfectibility of science, the book
works beautifully'
Elizabeth Buchan, *The Times*

'Complex and unusual . . . I found it impossible to
put down'
Barbara Erskine, *Sunday Express*

Christopher Wilkins was born in Oxford in 1945 and read English at King's College, Cambridge. He lives with his wife, Siân, in rural reclusion in the south of England. He is the author of *The Horizontal Instrument*.

The Poison Arrow Frog

Christopher Wilkins

Scribner

First published in Great Britain by Scribner, 2002
This paperback edition published by Scribner, 2003
An imprint of Simon & Schuster UK Ltd
A Viacom Company

Copyright © Christopher Wilkins, 2002

Scribner and Design are trademarks of
Macmillian Library Reference USA, Inc.,
used under licence by Simon & Schuster, the publisher of this work.

1 3 5 7 9 10 8 6 4 2

Simon & Schuster UK Ltd
Africa House
64–78 Kingsway
London WC2B 6AH

www.simonsays.co.uk

Simon & Schuster Australia
Sydney

A CIP catalogue record for this book is available from the British Library

ISBN 0-7432-0754-8

Typeset by Palimpsest Book Production Limited,
Polmont, Stirlingshire
Printed and bound in Great Britain by
Cox & Wyman Ltd, Reading, Berks

For Siân, again

Though blind to guilt, fate can
be merciless with the slightest
distractions.

Jorge Luis Borges

CHAPTER ONE

A still morning in late January with the dry season at its height and the sun well up in the sky. A lean and scabby dog with amber eyes slinks into the parched forecourt of a sprawling villa high in the hills above the old island capital, pausing to cock a sinewy leg against one of the desiccated wooden gateposts. Relieved, it slouches round towards the dustbins at the rear of the building, leaving a trail of drops pooling behind it in the grey dust like molten pewter. Before it can begin its investigation of the rubbish, the shutters of an upstairs corner window are flung wide, the clack and clatter sending flaky showers of turquoise paint spiralling down into the yard beneath, and the dog, spooked, flees the scene to resume its fussy downhill progress to the palm-dappled shade of the broad boulevards in the town below.

Moments later a second upstairs window creaks open at the opposite end of the building and, from these two dark apertures, a pair of maids poke out their heads and squawk loudly to one another in the impenetrable creole of the island.

1

These stolid domestics, sepia-skinned with random clumps of facial hair, function as the cockerels of the establishment, rousing from their often crapulent slumbers the last two permanent residents, who by dint of persistent and tedious negotiation now have their bedrooms at the rear of the building, on the western side untroubled by the rays of the rising sun.

Between those turquoise shutters, a blistered stucco the colour of apricots has selectively crumbled away over the years, leaving gaps the shape of almost-identifiable nations, exposing the tightly stacked bricks behind. Here and there across the façade are fragments of a rotting trellis to which clings an ancient and lethargic bougainvillea and, running the entire length of the building at the rear beneath the balconied windows of the still-drowsy occupants, is the veranda, creaking backdrop to decades of convivial sundowners, breathless rumours and the recriminatory conclusions to a thousand rubbers of bridge.

This, then, is *L'Auberge des Anglais*, as it has been known for the twenty or so years since it first opened its doors as a hotel and welcomed in those British colonial servants who felt themselves betrayed by the handing over of 'their' end of the island to the natives, yet who were reluctant to leave a part of the world they had come to look upon as home. For them, the Auberge was a refuge, a haven of Englishness on what was indisputable Gallic soil, the French having shrewdly and obstinately refused to bestow independence on their territory, granting it instead full status as an external *département* of France. The natives here in the eastern part of the island are as much citizens of France as are the natives of Normandie or the Haute-Savoie and are, for the most part, content with the arrangement.

After the maids, the next body to be restored to full consciousness is that of the mournful Gaston Delacroix, owner of the hotel. Hunched over his chipped and grimy marble washstand, he greets each bleary day with a yawning, hawking invective against whichever deity has decreed that he should spend his prime years as a hotelier – part waiter, part barman, all pimp, as he repeatedly puts it. He is a lanky stooping stork of a man and his face has the stretched sallow skin and honed beaky nose of the forest Indian. His is a face, as his wife never tires of telling you, which you could use to cut cane.

His ancestors of a mere four generations back wore no clothes and dwelt upriver in palm huts. The concept of work was unknown to his tribe, because the forest that sustained its members in all their needs made only minimal demands upon their energies. Fruit was abundant, fish were slow and gullible and the bulk of the day could be passed drowsing in

3

a hammock, smoking and getting gently drunk on *cachiri*. Today Gaston insists that his antipathy to labour is in his blood, that his indolence is not a failure of will on his part, but the legacy of his forebears.

His maternal grandmother had been a legendary whore in the old colonial days, and it was she who had changed the family name from its ungainly Indian form to Delacroix, following a visit to Paris where she had been much taken by that artist's painting of a tiger. The villa had been rented to her by a Dutch merchant, and her business had grown to the point where she had as many as thirty girls working for her. When the Hollander fell on hard times, she bought the house outright at a knockdown price, and ownership descended with the name through her unmarried daughter to the reluctant Gaston.

As he clambers into his clothes and shuffles across the back landing, his muttered curses bring his wife out of the kitchen below, where she has been toiling since before dawn, and she calls up to him in a strained whisper,

'We are all out of rum.'

He scratches himself dolefully and leans over the baluster rail to confront her. Magali Delacroix is a short, chunky woman with greying blonde hair and strong stubby hands presently covered in flour.

'What's that to me?' he answers. In the Auberge, by long-established convention, they speak to one another in the English patois of the native islanders, even though the language sits awkwardly in both their mouths.

'I'll tell you what that is to you, you worthless *mouton paresseux*.' She sets her foot on the bottom stair and he instinctively hunches his shoulders as though expecting a physical missile rather than a verbal onslaught. 'You and your "elegant" English friends have drunk all my kitchen rum.'

'Not possible,' he ventures, but he speaks hesitantly because the events of the previous night are returning to him.

'Then what has happened to it? Last night when I closed that kitchen door there was three quarters of a bottle of good Martinique rum on the table. Now there is no rum and no bottle.'

'The table's still there, then? That's something to be thankful for.'

She smiles in spite of herself and says,

'So what are you saying – we got ghosts? We got rum-swiggin' ghosts?'

'Could be, could be. Anyway, what for are you looking for rum at this time of the morning?'

'I have a fine gammon hock down here which needs marinating – as if it was any of your business.'

'I'll go check in the cellar. We got plenty, maybe.'

'Don't you go bringing me any of that rotgut grog. Martinique is what I want – what you owe me.'

Waving her away with a flap of his bony hand, he retreats back to the bedroom, muttering, 'Martinique, Martinique,' under his breath. He will get his wife her rum sooner, rather than later, because the curious fact is that he is secretly afraid of her. Though he is a veteran of the *Légion Etrangère*, and claims to have seen action at Ninh Phuoc and in Djibouti, he fears this dumpy woman with an irrational dread. It is nothing he can quite put his finger on – he cannot mentally conjure a situation in which she might do him real harm, but nonetheless the apprehension is there. He, who would without a moment's hesitation take on a machete-wielding intruder – as indeed he has done on at least two occasions – backs away at the first scent of conflict with this diminutive ironmonger's daughter from Marseille.

She returns to her kitchen, the one place in her narrow world where she can most nearly keep at bay the homesickness that constantly assails her. Here, at least, she can immerse herself in the exercise of her skills because Magali has a talent for cooking – a magnificent talent – and food is the mighty passion of her life. She does not know the source of her great gift. She can remember as a small child helping out in the kitchen of her uncle Laurent who served bouillabaisse from a caravan on the beach at Sète. She can recall the steam and sweat of the tin galley and the smell and stain of saffron on her fingers, but surely this distant experience alone cannot explain her love of cooking. As she sits herself down at the long, scoured kitchen table she gazes about her at the shimmering copper pans, the hanging bunches of herbs, the strings of onions and garlic, the glass jars of preserved vegetables and the earthenware crocks of good rich stock, and as she breathes in the breakfast aromas of bread and coffee, she feels herself deeply, deliriously embedded in her world.

The dining room bell tinkles high over the kitchen door, signalling that at least one of the residents has descended to take his *petit déjeuner*. Magali gets wearily to her feet and begins to prepare a tray. Almost without conscious thought, she allows her hands to build the familiar still-life arrangement of the two heavy silver jugs, the white bone-china bowl, the damask linen napkin, the plate, the knife and spoon, the twin dishes of butter – salted and sweet – the ramekin of *confiture d'abricots*. While she is ladling out the coffee and scalded milk, one of the maids enters the kitchen and waits wordlessly beside her until the tray is complete before hefting it shoulder high and bearing it off towards the dining room.

The only guest in evidence at this hour is Edward Arden

and he is seated in his habitual place, his chair facing outwards through the French windows, his gaze directed steadily at the table top before him. The clump of the maid's footsteps as she crosses the polished wooden floor does not provoke a reaction from him and as she lays out the breakfast, he does not look up. When she has completed her task only by the merest hint of a nod does he acknowledge her presence and she, with a muttered, '*Bon appetit*,' raises her eyes to the high, beamed ceiling, turns on her heel and leaves him to his thoughts.

This is not rudeness on his part, however, not some hauteur of the guest before the servant. The truth is that Edward Arden is afflicted with that least appealing of human frailties, shyness. He suffers, and has suffered all his life, from a debilitating self-consciousness in the presence of human society. With familiar faces he can, through strenuous effort, subdue the inner panic, but the mere thought of having to make a new acquaintance gives him palpitations of the heart and clammy palms. The prospect of encountering a group of strangers will drench his whole body in sweat, constrict his lungs and reduce him to a state of watchful paralysis. History does not celebrate the names of the shy. There is no Ivan the Timid for us to read about, no Mild Bill Hickock, and who would waste five minutes following the exploits of Richard *Coeur-de-Souris*? Those who suffer from the social vertigo we call shyness are as isolated as the deaf – more so, because they cannot help thrusting away those who would be close. It is like a self-inflicted leprosy, a defence against the world which the world in turn interprets as an insult. As the maid walks away from Arden's table in a huff, she cannot sense his discomfort. Even though she is as familiar to him as his own shoes, her daily approach can still bring a dryness to his mouth and a tremor to his hands.

In his sixty-third year, he is a slight, neatly dressed figure, still favouring the dapper formal day wear that was expected of him in the Foreign and Commonwealth service, where he served his long years as a translator, walling himself about with comforting, controllable words and shunning the company of unpredictable mankind. He is never without a pair of gold-rimmed reading spectacles which hang, when not in use, from a black silk moiré ribbon around his neck beneath that other visible idiosyncrasy, his moustache, a ragged, drooping effusion which gives his face a brooding, melancholy aspect. Those who do not know him – that is to say, almost everyone – see this hairy appendage as evidence of suppressed vanity, even of flamboyance, but the simpler truth is that he has very bad teeth and relies upon the moustache to conceal the fact from the world.

The pension he has built up, together with the allowances

he never spent, have ensured for him a secure future at the Auberge, where what he craves, above all, is routine and repetition. If he had his own way he would eat the same dishes at the same mealtimes each day, wear the same clothes, read the same edition of the same newspaper and retire to bed each night, having taken one third of a gill of whisky, on the dot of ten-thirty. He dreads novelty, forever quoting to himself the old Spanish prayer, 'God preserve us from all new things'. New situations startle him, new information confuses him and new people alarm him.

The only human being on the planet with whom he ever feels even partly at ease is the next to enter the dining room, a tall, heavily built man with an unruly mop of sandy hair and a ruddy, scraped complexion. A man who rubs his hands together a lot, and clasps your shoulder when he talks to you. A man who, though past fifty, still has the jaunty air of the lower school cricket captain.

CHAPTER TWO

D evenish is the name. Jack Devenish and I know exactly what you want to hear about. It's what they all want to hear about – the assassination. Well, I'll tell you one thing right off the bat, the whole business was a right bugger's muddle from start to finish, and there's no way anyone could have foreseen the way it would pan out. Not even yours truly, although looking back it all seems perfectly logical. What started the ball rolling was that woman arriving with the little piccaninny. No, I'm getting ahead of myself, where it all really started was at breakfast on the Tuesday morning. Arden was already in the dining room, dabbing that big droopy moustache of his with a napkin in that prissy way he had and I remember saying to him,

'Heard the latest, Ted?' Of course, he didn't say anything right off, because that's how he always was, bit standoffish, if you know what I mean. I was used to his manner by this time and never paid it any mind. To tell you the truth, I was quite fond of the old sod in those days, for all his peculiar ways. Of course that was before I found out just what a filthy degenerate bastard he

11

really was, under that meek and mild exterior. Anyway I went on, 'You'll never guess who's honouring us with his imperial presence for dinner next Saturday week. Eh? Any idea?' He looked across at me for a moment and shook his head. 'Only the big *cucaracha* himself from over the border. Only El Presidente – or whatever he's styling himself these days.'

'Here?' he sort of croaked, and I could see his left eyelid twitching away nineteen to the dozen. 'You mean President Bélizon is coming *here* – to this hotel? But this is the first I've heard of it.'

'Well, it would be,' I told him. 'It's all very hush-hush, top-secret, need-to-know basis. Apparently they've been planning it for months. Low-key visit, *entente cordiale* and all that malarkey. It's going to be a hell of a bash, by the sound of it.'

'But how do you know all this?' he said.

'Gaston told me last night. I poured the best part of a bottle of her ladyship's Martinique rum down him and he spilt the beans. And I've appointed myself chief of protocol, so you count on a couple of places for me and thee on the top table. Chance to get out your best bib and tucker – full dicky-bow job, I shouldn't wonder.'

'But the man's a monster, he's a fascist dictator. He's tortured and murdered God knows how many people.' D'you know, I'd never seen the old stoat so agitated.

12

'Be that as it may,' I told him, 'the French seem to think they can do business with him. There's some sort of trade delegation coming over from the old country. Something to do with bauxite or sugar or some such nonsense. I'm telling you, it's all planned from soup to nuts. And afterwards, there's going to be a socking great firework display.'

'How long's he staying?'

'Two nights, Friday and Saturday.'

'But why here? Why not down in the old Government House?'

'Simple,' I pointed out to him. 'Security. The French are terrified that someone's going to lob an iron pineapple through his bedroom window, so they're tucking him away up here in the hills. You could defend this place against an army, if it came to it.'

He looked doubtful, and perhaps I ought to proffer a word of explanation myself as to why such a scrofulous old pile should have been deemed appropriate accommodation for a visiting head of state. Fact of the matter is, that place had the best restaurant on the island. Probably the best in the whole of the Caribbean. It's what kept Gaston afloat, if you really want to know. You see, although the place started off as a simple dosshouse for retired old penpushers like me and Ted, gradually the business changed.

13

As Magali got into the swing of the *haute cuisine*, the scoff just got better and better. Soon, she was doing two sittings a night – one at seven for the residents – simple grub, but plenty of it – and another altogether more slap-up affair at nine for people up from town. As the number of residents tailed off, so she trained up more and more of the local lads as chefs and the restaurant business grew to the point where Ted and I were sitting down each night in a dining room stuffed with nothing but *la crème-de-la-crème* up from the old capital. And I was told by more than one visitor from France that the place would warrant a couple of rosettes in any restaurant guide, if only it were squatting in the suburbs of Lyon instead of being perched above some mosquito-infested tropical swamp. Still, it suited me.

Spot of local history now – can't be helped, if you want to get the whole picture. The western end of the island, which under British rule had been called Saint Peter, transformed itself in 1978 into the People's Republic of New Carabali. Which was a pretty good joke, given that it was run purely for the government and not for the people – which in my book disqualified it as a republic – and so far as anyone knew they had never held a single election.

The top biffo, President General Alphonse Bélizon, was some sort of military man with what you might call a mixed ancestry behind him. For some reason he felt a sort of affinity with the African slaves, which was why he called his own country after the millions of the poor buggers who had been shipped across from the Niger delta over the centuries. I suppose the name 'Liberia' had already been bagged and besides it might have looked too much like he was taking the piss, what with the total *lack* of liberty there seemed to be about the place.

There was only one pass through the central mountains and needless to say that was heavily guarded on both sides. Only difference was that the gendarmes on this side were there to keep people out, whereas his boys were trying to keep people in. Arden was right, of course. The papers were always full of atrocity stories about him and in the early days boatloads of poor devils kept washing up on the French side of the border, only to be shipped back to face God knows what grisly fate. They stopped coming after he crucified a bunch of them outside the presidential palace – no, literally – nailed them to the telegraph poles with his own hands, by all accounts. At least, that's what they said. Of course, you never know with atrocity stories, do you? People tend to exaggerate. In any event, it was donkeys' years since all that happened, when he was still a young man. Time we're talking about now, he was pushing seventy. Well past such fun and games.

When my breakfast coffee arrived that morning, Ted Arden had already worked himself up into a high old state. He jumped up from his table and started striding about with his hands stuck deep in his trouser pockets, muttering to himself over and over again, 'It can't be – it's not possible.' I said to him, 'Calm down, old son, it's only a meal. It'll be interesting, you'll see. I mean, when's the last time you sat down to dinner with an eighteen-carat international bastard? When did you last break bread with a certified mass murderer?' But he wasn't having any of it. Just shook his head and said,

'Sorry, but it's out of the question. Totally out of the question. The man's a monster, everybody agrees. I must talk to Gaston about this.'

'Talk as much as you like, old cock, it's a done deal. Highest level, sort of thing.'

'Totally unacceptable.'

And off he trotted to find *le patron*. I helped myself to his brioche and stuck my nose in the newspaper. I couldn't for the life of me figure out what he was getting so worked up about, but it's often the quiet ones you've got to watch, isn't it? That was shortly before *she* arrived and things would never be quite the same again for poor old Ted.

CHAPTER THREE

L ater that morning as Devenish wipes the last crumbs from his lips and carefully folds his three-day-old copy of the *Daily Telegraph*, his attention is caught by a taxi depositing its passengers at the Auberge's side door. They are a slender, austere-looking European woman dressed in black, and a small brown child of perhaps eight or nine, an Indian girl in a tattered cotton dress, shoeless and wide-eyed with wonder at the shabby grandeur of her surroundings. He watches with mounting curiosity as Gaston hurries out to offer a perfunctory greeting before hustling the pair briskly away towards the garden annexe. There is something in the way Gaston glances nervously about that smacks to Devenish of conspiracy, and if there is one thing Jack Devenish enjoys it is a spot of conspiracy.

As if by chance he sets off on a stroll around the grounds, and when his steps take him past the annexe, a rickety wooden bungalow hidden away amongst the dense shrubbery uphill from the main building, he cannot help but notice that

Gaston is busily occupied in closing all the shutters. Devenish pauses and lights a cheroot, making an extended, elaborate performance out of it in order to linger for as long as possible without betraying his interest. When Gaston spots him, there is a brief, awkward exchange of smiles before Devenish strolls slowly on, whistling quietly to himself.

He seeks out Magali in her kitchen and casually asks,

'So who's the *femme fatale* at the bottom of the garden?'

She pauses mid-way through filleting a bream and says,

'We may be goin' short of fish today. One of the boats didn't make it back to harbour this morning.' Hearing now what he said, she gives him a sharp look. 'What you talking about? What *femme*?'

'Gaston just took some young woman up to the annexe. She had a little girl with her. Little Indian girl.'

'Ah.' She stirs the air above her head with the filleting knife and sniffs contemptuously. 'That's one of Gaston's charity cases, I shouldn't wonder. Charity for him, more like.'

'So what's the scoop? What's the old rascal up to?'

'Best you don't ask. Certain sure best you don't find out.' She resumes her methodical work and Devenish saunters off to finish his cheroot on the veranda.

From where he sits he cannot quite see the annexe, but he knows that Gaston will have to pass him on his return to the

18

villa. It is not just that Jack Devenish wants there to be some mystery, he *needs* there to be. The ennui that suffuses his every waking moment has created in him an almost physical craving for incident. He is a man bored beyond endurance by the emptiness of his life and he is constantly on the qui vive for action. Retirement does not suit him. Temperamentally, he is a mirror image of Arden. His motto is 'anything but a quiet life'. Eventually Gaston reappears from the shrubbery and Devenish calls out to him,

'So who is she?'

The lanky hotelier hurries across the lawn, flapping an admonitory hand and hissing, 'Not so loud, not so loud. Keep your voice down.' He pulls up one of the whiskery rattan chairs and talks in a soft, earnest voice. 'That is Madame Lacombe and you are not to talk about her, if you please.'

'Fair enough,' Devenish says, '*I* won't talk about her. *You* talk about her.'

'It is a most sensitive business, you must understand. She is an angel, an angel of mercy. She is a very fine person, and I will not have her put at risk.'

Devenish lights another cheroot and says, 'My dear chap, I am, as you know, the soul of discretion. Anything you tell me will go no further.'

'No?' Gaston snorts. 'So how comes it that Monsieur Arden is chewing my ear this morning about the . . . the visit? How did he hear about that?'

'You don't have to worry about Ted, old bean. He's as discreet as the grave.'

'The grave is where I shall be in no time short with all these coming and goings.'

'So, what's the story?'

'*Eh bien*, you saw the little girl, yes? Well, it seems she is not entirely – how can I say – legally here. She does not exactly have the right documents to stay in the country. She is, as you might put it, a refugee.'

'From where?'

'Where do you think? Over the border. Madame Lacombe has rescued her. Which is all I need right now, I can tell you.'

'So how come you're involved?'

'Madame Lacombe is very,' he pulls the lobe of his ear in search of the word, 'persuasive.'

'You mean she's got something on you?'

Gaston wriggles in his seat. 'She has a number of friends who can behave on occasion in – unpredictable ways.'

'What d'you mean, gangsters? Terrorists?'

The other man winces. 'Men of principle, let us call them.'

'So how long's she going to be hiding here?'

'God knows. Couple of weeks maybe. Until she can buy some papers for the child.'

'Sounds highly dodgy to me. You want to watch your step, old son. Could all end in tears. Or jail.'

'I do not need you to be telling me this. My dear wife is a constant reminder. "Gaston," she says, "we could lose our livelihood over this." And I tell her, *I* could be losing something a lot more painful than that if I don't go along with this woman and her plans.' And with that lugubrious observation he gets wearily to his feet and shambles back into the Auberge.

Devenish finishes his cheroot and ponders over how he can turn this information to his advantage. When asked what he did in the old administration, he tends to lay a nicotine-stained finger alongside his nose and murmur something about, 'Cloak-and-dagger stuff,' hinting at some swashbuckling career in one of the intelligence branches. The truth is, he had been in overall charge of victualling the colonial residences, a post not without considerable opportunity for innovative book-keeping, of course, but hardly a job in which one was asked to take one's life in one's hands with any degree of regularity.

Long years of cooking the books have left him with an

eye to the main chance and a dowser's bump of location for the nearest cash register. It would also have left him with a considerable fortune of his own, had it not been for an unfortunate tendency towards optimism in the matter of racehorses. It seems to him that if Madame Lacombe has influential friends, and the kind of money it takes to procure forged papers, she is a lady with whom he might profitably become acquainted.

CHAPTER FOUR

That night, right after dinner, on the general principle that faint heart never won fair lady, I strolled over to her table and introduced myself. I could tell from the other side of the room that she was a handsome woman, but close up she was an absolute twenty-four-carat dazzler. She had long, coppery hair tied back in a sort of coil – like a Victorian governess. Her skin was almost luminous like thin Limoges china and she had enormous, almond-shaped eyes of the palest grey. Funny thing, though, about the eyes was, she had a slight squint, which in an odd sort of way served to emphasize the perfection of the rest of it. Quite taken aback I was, and a bit nonplussed in that way you are when you come across a real beauty. I stuck out my paw and managed to say,

'Devenish, at your service, ma'am. Jack Devenish.' Her hand felt quite cool, I remember, or maybe mine was just a bit warm. Anyway she said,

'How do you do, Mr Devenish? Diana Lacombe,' and she was English. I'd been expecting a bit of an uphill struggle with the language barrier, but no, she was as English as Berkeley Square. 'And this,' she went on, laying one of those cool hands on the little girl's arm, 'is Polly.' The child tucked her chin into her shoulder and looked down at the parquet.

'Perhaps,' I suggested, 'you might like to take coffee with me on the veranda?'

'That would be most pleasant, I'm sure, Mr Devenish.' So we went outside with the moppet in tow and settled down in a quiet corner.

'Have you come far?' she asked me, while one of the maids was pouring the coffee. I pointed up at the ceiling and confided that I too was a resident. 'How very fortunate you are,' she said, 'to be able to enjoy such exquisite food every day. The langouste was exceptional – Madame Delacroix is a true artist.'

'Are you staying with us long?' I asked.

'Do you know, I'm not entirely sure. I have a little business to transact, which may take some days.'

'And then back home, I suppose?'

'I do not really have a home in that sense. Not since my husband died.'

'Forgive me,' I blustered, 'I had no intention of . . .'

'Please don't feel awkward, Mr Devenish. No, since Didier's death I have led a somewhat peripatetic existence. I stay mostly in small hotels like this.'

'Do you not want to settle somewhere?'

'Not for the moment. For the moment, I enjoy living the life of a nomad. I like never having to clean the bath.'

I'm bound to say, the sudden unexpected vision of her getting out of a bath brought a flush to my cheeks. I'll swear she knew what I was thinking, too, by the way she laughed and patted me gently on the hand.

'But you, living here as you do, do you not feel rootless?'

'Me? Lord, no. This is tailor-made for a chap like me. It's a bit quiet sometimes but by and large this place is just the ticket. Just what the doctor ordered. Talking of which, can I tempt you to a *digestif* of some sort? A cognac, maybe? Or they have some excellent rum here – Martinique, 25-year-old.'

'I won't, thank you, Mr Devenish, but I would enjoy seeing you drink one. And I noticed earlier in the day that you smoke cigars. Please do not forbear on my part. I adore the aroma of a good cigar.'

What a woman, eh? That's what I was thinking to myself. The rum turned up and I treated myself to a Montecristo number two – the old torpedo. Only nigger in the ointment was Ted who chose that moment to appear and settle himself down at the next table – well within earshot – to read the local rag. Cramped the old Devenish style more than somewhat, I can tell you. And then something very odd happened. The moppet, who'd been hanging on to Diana's arm and generally lolling about like a damp dishcloth, detached herself and went over to Ted's table, where she flopped into the chair beside him and poked her head up between the newspaper and his face, gawping at him with a daft grin. He froze like a rat cornered by a snake, staring down at her, and then she slowly reached up with both hands and grabbed hold of his moustache. Not hard, but she gave it a definite tug. He went several shades of aubergine and Diana was up like a shot, scooping the child into her arms and saying,

'I am most terribly sorry about that. I'm afraid we've got ourselves a little over-excited today. New surroundings and one thing and another. Please accept my apology. I'm sure Polly would apologize for herself, but I'm afraid she doesn't speak very much proper English. In fact, she doesn't really speak any.'

Arden leapt up to apologize in turn to her, although what he'd got to be sorry about, I couldn't for the life of me fathom. I think apologizing was a kind of reflex with Ted. When in doubt, apologize. I saw that it was time to take control of the situation.

'Ted,' I said, pushing back my chair, 'let me introduce you. This is Madame Diana Lacombe. Madame Lacombe, *je vous présente* Edward Arden, late of Her Majesty's Service.' They shook hands and she invited him to join us, which was a bit rich I thought, given that everything seemed to be going on my tab, but what can you do? After plenty of, 'I couldn't possibly intrude' and a fair bit of, 'don't give it another thought', Ted was persuaded to pull up a stool and order himself a large malt. I noticed that Diana was keeping a tight grip on the moppet, who was still finding the whole incident hugely funny, gurgling to herself and eyeing Ted's moustache for all the world like she was planning a repeat performance.

'So you too are a resident here, Mr Arden?' Diana asked him.

'Yes, yes. Very much so. It suits me, d'you see? Suits me down to the ground. Couldn't be better from my point of view. All the comforts of home, so to speak. Except that I never really had much of what you'd call a home. Not really . . .' And he sort of tailed off. Typical of Ted. Most of the time you couldn't get two joined-up words out of him, then suddenly he'd be rambling on like a drunk on a bus. She smiled at him in a kindly sort of a way and said,

'As I was telling Mr Devenish earlier, I too am something of a homeless creature. Something of a rootless wanderer.'

'Quite, quite,' he gabbled, 'any place I hang my hat is home. It's all one to me. Well, lovely meeting you.' He knocked back

27

his whisky, sprang up with such vigour that the backs of his knees collided with the stool and sent it skittering off along the deck, turned beetroot again, shook hands briskly with Diana and fled the scene of the crime. As I was retrieving the wayward piece of furniture Diana stood up and I was in there like greased weasel shit.

'Walk you to your door,' I said, 'no trouble. It's tricky in the dark if you're not familiar with the lie of the land.' She gave me a quizzical sort of a look and said,

'Most considerate of you, Mr Devenish.'

'Jack, please. I insist you call me Jack.'

'Thank you, Jack.' She scooped up the little'un and let me take her elbow and steer her through the oleanders to her front door. What transpired thereafter, it would be ungallant of me to relate.

CHAPTER FIVE

The path from the veranda steps to the annexe is short, free from natural hazards and at night is clearly illuminated by a series of electric lamps concealed at ground level in the shrubbery. As they arrive, Devenish lets his grasp slip from elbow to hand and, raising that cool appendage to his lips, plants a kiss upon the back of it, a kiss which is both firmer and more prolonged than might be felt customary after so brief an acquaintance. She waits for her hand to be released but he continues to hold on until she leans forward and whispers, in a voice that slips into his ear like an ice pick,

'Don't push your luck, Jacky boy.'

He drops her hand as though it were a live viper and takes an involuntary backward step, raising his own hand in mock salute.

'Got the picture,' he raps out cheerily. 'Overstepped the mark, there. Hope to get better acquainted. Sleep tight.' He extends his hand again, this time intending to ruffle the child's hair, but she shrinks away from him and seeks refuge in her guardian's shoulder. With a shrug, he turns away and makes his way back to the veranda. Any observer who had chanced to be standing concealed in the bushes as he passed would have heard him utter the simple phrase,

'Bugger it.'

Mid morning on the following day, Magali is at her duties in the kitchen, dismembering a goat. As she works, she listens to an old and treasured cassette of the ballads of her beloved Georges Brassens, whose sonorous Marseillais rumble with its exaggeratedly rolled 'r's never fails to transport her, moist-eyed, back to the people and landscape of her childhood. When Brassens died, she said it was worse for her than losing a member of the family. 'There's always more family,' she would say, 'but there was only one Brassens.' The song that presently engages her is one she finds almost unbearably poignant – '*Supplique pour être enterré à la plage de Sète*' – the troubadour's mesmerically haunting testament written in the autumn of his life, his plaintive request to have his body trans-ported, '*Dans un sleeping du Paris-Méditerranée / Terminus en gare de Sète*', there to be buried on the beach under his '*sol natal*'. She plays the tape at maximum volume on an ugly portable music centre that squats on its high shelf like a dusty black toad. The tape is now so worn and frayed from constant replaying that the sound sizzles and pops, but she would not have it any other way. The music's decay is part of her nostalgia, part of her continuing loss. She sings along to her favourite verse, the 'shipwreck', a gentle smile in her eyes as she intones the familiar lyrics: '*Le capitaine cri: «Je suis le maître à bord! Sauve qui peut! Le vin et le pastis d'abord! Chacun sa bonbonne et courage!»*' There is something so blissfully anarchic to her in these words, something so '*Marseillais*' – never mind the women and children, save the wine and the pastis – she loves the melancholia in this music and the mischief.

Gaston shambles into the kitchen and she stops singing. She suspects that he does not appreciate Brassens, though he would never dare pass comment, much less suggest turning down the volume. He crosses to the tall pine dresser and, taking a tiny brass key from his pocket, unlocks the right-hand drawer. Magali glares at the back of his neck as he takes out a grubby towelling bundle, pulls up a seat at the opposite end of the kitchen table from her, and begins unfolding the package as carefully as a new mother removing a baby's nappy. Inside is his most revered possession, his gun. It is no ordinary gun, he will have you know. It is nothing less than a Desert Eagle. Nor is it any ordinary Desert Eagle, he will further inform you, but a Desert Eagle with the special extended 356mm barrel.

'What for you want to be foolin' around with that thing

31

now?' Magali shouts across to him. 'Too much to ask you maybe going to blow your brains out?'

'Too small a target for me,' he calls back. 'Easy miss.' They exchange weary smiles, each of them taking comfort from this ritual exchange of threadbare badinage. He picks up the weapon and sniffs it, luxuriating in its oily, metallic reek. The pistol is a trophy, he will tell you proudly, with the implication that he prised it from some lifeless enemy fist on the bloody field of battle. In truth he stole it in Sidi-bel-Abbès from a semi-comatose Belgian mercenary who passed out during a heated and acrimonious dice game, over the course of which Gaston had plied him mercilessly with both kif and arak.

It is a beautiful thing to behold, he thinks, this gun – the first automatic pistol built to cope with the firing stresses of a magnum round. So great is the force of the charge that even a so-called 'non-lethal' hit can knock over and disable a target through simple traumatic shock. In the hands of an experienced combat veteran it is a very dangerous weapon indeed. It is more dangerous still in the hands of an untrained recruit. So great is the power of the recoil, it can dislocate the unwary shoulder. Its noise is deafening, its flash is blinding. It is a massive, ludicrous piece of artillery.

'Politics, that's what I'm thinking about,' he tells his wife as he sets about stripping the gun down. 'Soon we're going to have a whole bucketful of politics in this house and I'm taking no chances.'

The tape comes to an end and in the gluey silence that follows, she asks him,

'What in Jesus' name you got to do with politics? What you ever know about politics?'

'I tell you what I know, woman. When politics comes round the corner, there's going to be somebody shooting somebody someplace soon.'

'And it's going to be you, I suppose, doin' the shootin'?' She hacks at the goat with her cleaver, then prises open the hip joint with a thin stiff blade and wrenches off one of the hind legs. It makes a noise, *schlop*, like a boot freed from heavy mud. He winces.

'I have the right to defend myself and my family.'

'Against who exactly you plannin' to defend us all? You think President Bélizon is coming here to rape and murder us all in our beds? He's coming to eat some good food, is all.'

'That may be so. Maybe so. But he won't be coming on his own, will he? He not going to turn up on his *mobylette*, roll up his sleeves and say, "Where's me dinner, woman?", is he? There'll be all sorts with him. Troops, spooks, God only knows what scum and riffraff. What I'm saying is he'll have a whole fuckin' *entourage* with him.'

33

Magali stops her work and stares at him. She shakes her head slowly and jabs the severed goat leg in his direction, emphasizing her words.

'*You* are crazy. You really are crazy. They will lock you up.'

He shrugs but says nothing more, busying himself with the dismantled gun, oiling the parts and reassembling them with the methodical patience of a seasoned campaigner. He empties the magazine, carefully checking all seven rounds, and replaces them, relishing the steely click as each one slots into place. The first time he fired the gun he had hiked over to a secluded beach on the Algerian coast during his *Légion* days and even though he braced himself wide-legged in the sand, using a double-handed grip, the recoil knocked him staggering back and it was minutes before he could hear the screams of the infuriated seagulls circling overhead. With practice, he came to learn the knack of it and was able to hit even quite distant targets with tolerable accuracy. He would pick a mark on the crumbling rock face behind the beach and whoop with delight when it vanished in a cloud of orange dust and rubble, leaving behind a crater the size of a dustbin lid. Once in the Kaçkar Mountains he had shot a ram mouflon, hitting the beast in the neck. The head had sailed off into a ravine, leaving the body standing foursquare on a ledge, a fountain of blood arching from the ragged wound.

He finishes loading the magazine, slaps it into place with the heel of his hand and, after giving the weapon a final smear of oil, rewraps it and locks it away again in its drawer. Magali crosses to the music centre, turns the cassette over and resumes her labours on the goat. Gaston gives her a lopsided grin and wanders out to stand on the back step. Blinking in the sunlight, he thrusts his hand deep inside his trousers and rummages about in his groin. Raising his fingers absent-mindedly to his great beak, he savours the aromatic cocktail of gun oil and unwashed flesh.

CHAPTER SIX

Damnedest thing I ever saw, the way the little coon cub took to Ted Arden. After a couple of days, they were well-nigh inseparable and, of course, everywhere the little one went, Diana went too. Which, as you can imagine, put a sizeable damper on any amorous plans I'd been entertaining in that direction. Talk about a chap coming out of his shell – Arden was for all the world like a great big kid himself. The day after the moustache incident, he made a doll for the moppet. Made it out of a big old clothes peg and one of those padded satin coat hangers. Made the thing a little frilly frock and everything – cut it out of some scraps of cloth he'd dug up from somewhere – one of his old shirts, I shouldn't wonder. Anyway, the little'un was tickled pink with the thing and kept hugging and kissing it and talking to it in some heathen forest argot. The three of them took to sitting out in front of the annexe like one of those ghastly happy families on the old railway posters. It made you want to vomit. Well, it did me, anyway.

Mind you, it wasn't as though I didn't have enough on my plate, helping Gaston see to all the arrangements for the state visit. He wasn't altogether convinced he needed my help to begin with, mind you, but I pretty soon persuaded him he'd be out of his depth without my input. Seriously out of his depth.

'Protocol, for instance,' I pointed out to him. 'How well up are you on diplomatic protocol?' Of course he knew as much about diplomatic protocol as I know about veterinary dentistry, namely half the square root of sod all. 'I mean,' I said, 'just an apparently harmless decision like who sits next to who is fraught with peril. Fraught with it. You put the wrong bum on the wrong seat and you could have a major international incident on your hands.' That wiped the smile off his face pretty sharpish, I can tell you. 'No, my fine-feathered friend,' I reassured him, 'you put yourself in the capable hands of Jack Devenish. Leave the cooking to the lady wife and the protocol to me, and it'll all go off swimmingly.' By this point in the conversation he'd broken out in a muck sweat.

'I tell you, Jack, I swear to God I could do without all this shit coming down on me right now.'

'Don't give it a moment's further thought, *mon brave*. Diplomacy is second nature to the Devenish clan. Mother's milk.'

Which is how he and I came to be standing side by side outside the Auberge's guest entrance a couple of days later when a shiny black Citroën swept in and disgorged as weird a couple of specimens as you'd ever care not to meet in a dark alley. Specimen number one was a little roly-poly fellow of about forty in a dark suit and patent leather shoes. His hair was plastered down on his scalp in a glossy black slick, which together with the shoes gave you the impression that he'd been polished at both ends. The other character was a lot younger and must have been well over six foot in his socks. He was all tricked out in what looked like desert camouflage gear. His hair was dead white and cropped so close to his head it looked like he'd been left out overnight in a heavy frost and he was wearing these tiny little round sunglasses, which made his eyes look really close together.

The one in the suit presented himself to us in faultless English as Monsieur Christian Guitry 'from the Ministry in Paris' – though which ministry, he didn't bother divulging to us lesser mortals. He then introduced the big bastard as Captain Van der Pump, who promptly stuck out his hand and said, in an accent that reeked of the veldt,

'A great pleasure, gentlemen, I'm sure,' while giving the impression that it was nothing of the sort. His hand felt like a pine plank. 'I am here at the kind invitation of the French authorities to check out the security situation regarding the forthcoming presidential visit.' He turned and looked back at the gateposts through which they'd just arrived and asked, 'Is that the only road up to this place?' Gaston nodded. 'And where does it lead to beyond here?'

'Nowhere much,' I told him. 'It sort of peters out into the hills.'

'There are no more houses up there?'

'None that I'm aware of.'

He nodded sharply, as though those were the very words he'd been hoping to hear.

'We'll need to put an armoured car up there. There's nowhere really to set down a chopper, so we'll have to bring him in by road.' He turned to Guitry and said, 'I reckon forty men should just about do it, if that's acceptable.'

Gaston looked uncomfortable.

'Might I inquire,' he asked in a wheedling sort of voice, 'where these men will be expected to sleep?'

Van der Pump took off the dark glasses, which gave me a distinctly queasy turn, and no mistake. His eyes were pale pink, like an Angora rabbit's. He was an albino.

'Don't concern yourself with such matters, Mr Delacroix,' he said with a bleak smile, slapping about half a hundred-weight of hand on Gaston's shoulder, 'you won't be expected to cater for them. We'll camp some place up the road. Set up a field kitchen. You will of course be expected to accommodate the President's personal guards, but there will only be three of them, so you shouldn't find your resources unduly overstretched.' He seemed to enjoy using expressions like 'unduly overstretched' and 'regarding the forthcoming visit'. He talked like he'd learned English by post.

'And might *I* inquire,' I said to him, 'purely out of academic interest, who exactly it is that you're working for?' He spun round at this and fixed me with a stare that tied a round turn and two half-hitches in the old scrotum.

'What did you say?' he asked very quietly.

'Just curious, old man,' I managed to squeak.

'None of your fucking business,' he said after what felt like about an hour and a half.

'Quite right,' I told him. 'Get your drift.'

The little bureaucrat jumped in at this point and said,

'Captain Van der Pump is on secondment to the French security forces. I can vouch for him unconditionally.'

'Oh, yes,' I thought to myself, 'and who vouches for you, sunbeam?' But what I said was, 'Well, that's all right, then.'

'You'd better believe it,' said the good Captain, and he and the man from the Ministry toddled off to recce the grounds with Gaston trolling along behind them like a loyal hound.

I left them all to it. As far as I was concerned they could stew in their own juice. Any man who can't keep a civil tongue in his head forfeits the respect of Jack Devenish, I can tell you.

CHAPTER SEVEN

H idden high in the rocks above the Auberge there is a
pool, constantly replenished by a mountain rill that
passes through on its seabound course from the snowy central
peaks. The pool is deep and large enough for swimming and
the water, icy cold whatever the season, is pure enough to
drink. It has long been a cherished haunt of Edward Arden's,
a refuge which remains his secret because although it is a
mere twenty minutes' scramble up the hillside, the way to
it is tortuous and difficult to discern. The tranquillity of
the situation, the almost subliminal plash of the stream, the
resinous scent of the pines, the cool viridian shadows cast on
the water by the rock walls, can all be relied upon to soothe his
nerves and restore his inner sense of self. Others, he supposes,
must know of the spot, but he has never met anyone else there
and has found no evidence of the presence of mankind.

Until the arrival of Diana Lacombe, he has never spoken of
the pool to a living soul, for fear of having its solitude contam-
inated by the presence of another. Now, three days after her

arrival, they are sitting together on a flat basalt slab, shaded by lush conifers, watching the slender, naked Polly plunge repeatedly into the crystalline water. She has found the perfect overhanging rock from which to launch herself, and as her confidence grows, she leaps ever higher, her outstretched limbs spelling a brief letter 'X' in the air before she drops, legs pedalling furiously like a cartoon cat striving to outrun gravity. Each time her grinning face breaks the surface of the water she pauses only to suck in a couple of shivery breaths before striking out once more for the shore, sleek and swift as an elver.

'Such happiness,' Arden remarks.

'Oh, I cannot tell you how much it raises my spirits to see her like this,' Diana tells him. 'She has been through so much, there has been so little joy in her life. And now look at her – she is a child again, a real child.'

'A child *again*, you say?'

'Yes, I did, didn't I? Well, she has had little enough childhood. You would not believe the condition in which I found her, Mr Arden. You could not begin to imagine the squalor and degradation, the brutality and hardship she has had to endure.'

'And is she now really free of it all, do you think? From what you tell me, there is still some risk of her being sent back, if things don't work out with the immigration people here.'

'Oh, have no fears on that score. I've sprinkled more than

enough money about to keep the right wheels oiled. My late husband taught me a great deal about how to get things done in this wicked world.'

'You see it as a wicked world?'

'Don't you?'

'I don't suppose I do, really,' Arden confesses, after a moment's reflection. 'I've always seen the world as a pretty benign sort of place. Of course, wicked things happen – you read about them all the time – but mostly, I think people are essentially good.'

'Even President Bélizon?'

A shadow of bitterness crosses Arden's face and he says, turning away,

'He is an evil man.'

'My, my, Mr Arden, you speak as though you know that for a fact.'

'I do. I have good reason to know it.'

'You astonish me. What dealings can you possibly have had with Alphonse Bélizon?'

'It is an old story,' he begins, but his voice falters and he murmurs, 'but not one that I am yet ready to tell, I'm afraid. Forgive me.'

She pats his hand and they watch in silence as Polly takes yet another shrieking plunge into the pool.

'What do you know,' she asks him eventually, 'about the poison arrow frog?'

'Not a thing,' he admits, startled by the apparent change of topic.

'It lives in the rainforests of the mainland and the female of the species has developed the most extraordinary way of bringing up her young. When the tadpoles hatch from the eggs, she sticks one to her back using some kind of secreted mucus. Then she climbs high up into the forest canopy and deposits it into one of the pools of water that collect round leaf joints. Again and again she does this, one tadpole at a time. She returns each day to feed them until they become viable frogs, and do you know what she feeds them *on*?' Arden shakes his head. 'She feeds them on her own unfertilized eggs. Is that not admirable, Mr Arden? Is that not truly admirable?'

'I've never heard anything like it.'

'I see myself as that mother frog. Polly is just one of my tadpoles, one of my little black tadpoles that I have carried to safety. I call them all Polly – it makes them that much harder for wicked men to trace.'

'How many have there been?'

'Seven. This is my seventh little Polly.'

'But we have never seen you here before at the Auberge, I believe?'

46

'No,' she smiles bleakly, 'things did not go according to plan on this occasion. From the beginning, I always brought them out by boat – I am a more than competent mariner – and we would put to sea while it was still dark – half an hour or so before first light – and I made sure never to carry a radar reflector. Each little Polly I transferred close inshore to the smack of a local sympathizer – a fisherman. I myself had always needed to return, lest I be missed later at the border check when I left the country officially. I have dual nationality, you see. My husband was Canadian so I have a Canadian passport, which allows me pretty fair access, but it would be dangerous to abuse that privilege.

'Anyway, this time we were unlucky – or perhaps betrayed. A heavy mist rolled in just as we were nearing the rendezvous point and when we hove to we could hear the engines of what must have been a patrol boat. We sat there, shivering in the mist, and then we heard heavy machine-gun fire but without being able to tell which direction it was coming from – you know what it's like in the mist. I tell you, Mr Arden, it was absolutely terrifying. I was convinced we were going to die. Then the patrol boat moved away until we could no longer hear it and all we could do was wait until the sun burnt off the mist. We found the fishing boat drifting about a quarter of a mile from us but when we reached her there was nobody on board and she was full of blood. The radar reflector was at the masthead.

'I brought her in under tow and took Polly straight to my hotel room in Belleville, but after we had dried ourselves and I had changed my clothes, I knew that it would be unsafe for either of us to stay there, even for a day. I had been given Gaston's name by our fisherman sympathizer, and so here we are.'

'And you believe that it was you they were looking for? You say you might have been betrayed?'

'I think it's possible. In any event, it will be my last such expedition. The situation is becoming far too dangerous. I do not lack courage . . .'

'I should say not.'

'. . . but there are limits to what is sensible and practical. So, over there you see my last little Polly.'

Arden looks across to where the child is poised on tiptoe at the edge of her rock, arms uplifted to the sky. Her wet skin seems to shimmer in the reflected sunlight and he notices the two perfectly symmetrical dimples either side of her spine just above the buttocks. Without any voluntary effort of thought he finds himself imagining the sensation of cupping those slender haunches in his hands and placing his thumbs in those twin smooth hollows. His conscious mind traps and examines the notion and he is instantly appalled. A feeling of nausea rises in him and, flushed and trembling, he jerks his gaze away. Diana, shading her eyes against the glare, sees nothing untoward.

CHAPTER EIGHT

It was my habit in those days, of a Saturday night, to take a jaunt down into the old port to a waterfront bar called *Le Macaque Agile* where the weekly congregation would sink a few companionable tinctures before assembling in the upstairs room for a quiet game of cards. The stakes weren't particularly high, but a fellow who kept his wits about him could come away with a decent wad of walking-around money. The owner was a swarthy little one-eyed Armenian called Alfie Petrosian and he kept it as a hobby, rather than for gain. He had no need to run the place at a profit, on account of his principal trade being rum-running out of Nassau with just the occasional diversification into smuggling tractor parts into Cuba.

Although he was hardly tall enough to cut cabbage, he drove this sodding great yellow Hispano-Suiza, built in 1926 with scarlet leather upholstery. He'd treat you to a ride at the drop of a hat, but nobody ever took him up on the offer twice. He had problems, you see, judging distances with that one eye and a trip up into the mountains with

51

Alfie at the wheel could turn your hair white at the first
bend.

The bar was a smoky, insalubrious kind of a dive with
festoons of dusty polythene lianas hanging down the walls,
and a glazed tile floor underfoot that would all but disappear
by chucking-out time, buried in deep drifts of cigarette butts.
During the day the place was dark and clammy, like the cave
of some hibernating beast, but at night it was drenched in
light from long fluorescent tubes that flickered and hurt your
eyes to look at. There were big ceiling fans that circled slowly
overhead like buzzards but they hardly began to stir the fug.

The furniture was all bent chrome, the chairs laced through
with plastic imitation raffia the colour of pus. In the small
back room was a battered old *baby-foot* table into which
quartets of off-duty gendarmes would drop their small change
and fag ash and when you went to the gents there was
this raddled old macaw on a perch over the door who sat
blinking innocently at the assembled company, waiting to
entertain them by crapping on your head when you came
out. The bird was rumoured to have been working on the
trick for more than seventy years. In fact, the only item
on the premises under forty years old was a monstrous
great Bang & Olufsen television set in the far back corner
which, although it was brand-new, was apparently incapable

of receiving anything but Italian soccer matches and baseball games from Havana.

That Saturday, a week before the presidential visit, the devil had decided that his pasteboards were to fall my way all night. An hour into the session I was already nineteen hundred francs to the good, which was over two hundred quid in coin of the realm. In addition to the usual bunch of reprobates, the game had managed to attract a genuine, copper-bottomed imbecile in the shape of a young student named Jay Horowitz, a chubby Californian with a bad perspiration problem and the smirky face of a pig who'd just remembered a dirty joke. His rich daddy, he told us all proudly, in order to broaden his horizons had dispatched him off round the world with a backpack full of condoms and clean socks, and an American Express gold card. This prize tosser, having stood us all a couple of hefty rounds of rum punches, went on to profess himself to be 'something of a connoisseur' (he pronounced it like 'sewer') when it came to the game of poker. Not to take advantage of such a pluckable fowl would, of course, have been contrary to the laws of nature, and Jack Devenish is nothing if not a stickler for the laws of nature.

Seven of us sat down at the table that night and when we got up three hours later six of us were in profit, glory be. Young Horowitz, we calculated afterwards, had pissed away something like eighteen hundred US dollars. Hard cash, too – no markers. Every time he ran out of folding money, Alfie would run that gold card through the machine, pass over a roll of bills and off we'd go again.

We did not, I will have you know, chisel the poor bastard. I'm bound to admit there was the occasional spot of sand-bagging, the odd big-dog-little-dog flanker, and at one point somebody or other – might even have been me – pulled the old Kentucky blaze on the poor sod. No, we didn't cheat him, but that was only because we didn't need to. His ruin was all of his own making. He had that miraculous combination – happily common in the young – of arrogance and ignorance, which in a game of chance inevitably leads to a healthy redistribution of wealth.

Funny thing was how he took it all in such good part, laughing and joking right the way through, ordering up more drinks and roaring with delight when anyone raked in a particularly juicy pot. Maybe he was even richer than we thought. Maybe he was so rich that he didn't give a monkey's how much he lost. No matter. Point is, he'd set me up with the wherewithal to pay a little call on a recent acquaintance of mine, and that's what I really had in mind to tell you about.

Hortense was the friend's name and she was – not to put too fine a point on it – a lady of easy virtue. A woman of the night. On the game. What I mean is that if you gave her the money, she'd give your willy a damn good licking. I'm not bragging about the arrangement, but I'm not ashamed of it, either. Ask most fellows if they've ever been with a hooker and they'll swear blind they've never so much as clapped eyes on one. 'I've never had to pay for it in my life' is the kind of bollocks that gets trotted out whenever the subject of tarts comes up at the nineteenth hole. It's a miracle, when you come to think about it, that the trade has survived all these centuries. I mean, reckon it up for yourself. Scrubbers in every colour of the rainbow hanging it out for sale from Anchorage to Alice Springs. Thousands, maybe millions, of them and not a single paying customer in sight. Beats me how they manage to make ends meet.

Anyway, so far as I was concerned, Hortense was the answer to an old bachelor's prayer and worth every sou. She was some sort of mulatto, I suppose – half-caste, octoroon, whatever you want to call it – and she was long and slinky and her heels jutted out over the backs of her sandals, the way black girls' feet always seem to. Hardly any tits to speak of, but an arse on her like a pair of ripe cantaloupes. Thick wedge of frizzy hair sticking forward like a peaked cap over these great big watery eyes and a pair of lips you could use for a sink plunger.

Pleased to see me? You bet she was pleased to see me,

'specially when I showed her the colour of Jay Horowitz's money. Being flush like I was, it seemed the decent thing to spread it around a bit, so I slipped her double the usual rate and lay back while she did her best work. God, I have to tell you it was a real tonic to watch the glorious dusky orbs of her bum jostling together right up there in front of my face while she did the business on the old man with the India rubber gobbling gear.

The other great thing I have to say about Hortense is that she wasn't one of these blasé, 'just leave the money on the mantelpiece will you dearie I haven't got all night you know?' sort of tarts. Know what I mean? Some of them never let you forget that it's just a commercial transaction to them. Inverted snobbery sort of thing – 'I may be an old slapper,' you can see them thinking, 'but at least I'm not a poor sad punter like you.' Takes all the romance out of the thing, to my way of thinking, like paying your dentist to give you one off the wrist. Hortense wasn't like that at all. She was someone you could have a real conversation with. You may laugh, but I'm serious; she was a really interesting person in a great many ways.

After she'd drained me drier than a lizard's fart, we cracked open the bottle of Wild Turkey I'd brought along, and sat looking out of the windows, breathing in the cool air and listening to the street sounds of late-night revellers tumbling home to their beds.

'Tell me something, Hortense,' I said to her. 'Where do you stand on this chap Bélizon?'

She exploded with laughter, her lips spraying a fine mist of whiskey all over her satin wrap.

''bout far away as my skinny long legs will carry me. That man gives me the screamin' abdabs, stories you hear about him and all his dirty doin's.'

'You know he's coming here next weekend?'

'I heard talk of it.'

'You ever go back across the border?'

'Only ever cross that border in the one direction – when I was fifteen and my uncle Silas brung me across in a truckload a yams. He paid off one of the border guards, which I heard got disappeared shortly after.'

'Never knew that.'

'Certain thing. That's how I got into this sorry trade. My uncle wanted I should pay back all the bribe money and he figured to take it all in kind – like, y'know, screwin' me whenever he got the urge. Trouble was, the urge didn't visit him that often 'cos he was an old geezer and his bits and pieces didn't always work like they should of. He finally done the calculation and says to me one day, "Hortense, way we

goin' on, I be dead and buried 'fore I halfway through getting my money back. We'd best find you some paying customers."
So I started puttin' out for his drinkin' buddies, which weren't too bad, considerin' – they was all pretty kind to me and I got to keep some of the money, buy myself some nice things to wear. Went on for a year or so, then the old lunatic got himself killed in a knife fight by some crazy Bajan used to share his teeth with.'

'Run that past me again,' I said, the bourbon singing in my ears. 'What do you mean, "share his teeth"?'

'What I say. They got this one set of dentures between them, save money. Take it in turns, week in, week out. Well, one day the Bajan tells uncle Silas 'bout how his daughters are proposin' to throw this big birthday party for him – sixtieth birthday it was, and Silas was invited all right – only the day it was all planned for happened to fall durin' Silas's week for the teeth. So the Bajan asks if maybe they can do a swap, like change the schedule, so's he can enjoy the steak dinner they all got planned for him. Silas tell him, birthday or no birthday, a deal is a deal and no way is he, Silas, going to sit down to no steak dinner without those teeth, and that's how it starts. Pretty soon the Bajan's wavin' this blade around and Silas is mockin' him somethin' chronic, takin' out the false gnashers and rattlin' them in the air like castanets, so the Bajan sticks him in the neck and five minutes later, it's "goodnight Guadeloupe".'

'So why did you still carry on working after he died?'

'Well, you know how it is, you get used to anything, keep at it long enough. I tried one or two what you might call "straight jobs" but somehow I didn't never get to settlin' in. 'Sides, I'd built up quite a regular "*clee-on-tell*" by this time, and seein' as how all that money rollin' in was mine all mine, seemed fool crazy to quit. And every now and then I get to do some bit of charity work with the money and that makes me feel good about meself, you know?'

'Charity work? What kind of charity work?'

She gave a shrug and took a long gargle of whiskey. 'You wouldn't believe me if I tell you.

'Anyways, why you asking about that old rascal Bélizon?' she asked after a while.

'They're giving a banquet for him up at the Auberge next weekend,' I told her, 'and I was wondering if you would do me the honour of being my guest?'

She looked as if somebody had smacked her on the back of the head with a monkey wrench and I suppose you might be wondering yourself what could have possessed me to invite such a creature to a formal state banquet. Fact of the matter is, I was rather keen to show Hortense off to Madame la-di-da

Lacombe. In my experience, there's nothing like a comely rival appearing on the scene to make a woman hot to drop her drawers for you. I wanted her to see that, far from being the desperate old lecher he might appear, Jack Devenish was by no means short of a place to park his plonker come bedtime.

'Me?' said Hortense, her eyes popping out of her head. 'You want to take me to a banquet? You askin' me to sit down at table with the evil one, the devil incarnate?' She poured herself another three fingers and grinned. 'Hey, you know what? Might be fun at that. Any case, I'm a sucker for a banquet. Shit, you know me – I'm a sucker for two hundred francs.'

On my way out I bumped into Guitry on the stairs. He had his chin tucked down and although he gave me a sideways sort of a glance, I couldn't tell if he recognized me. I wondered if he was on his way up to see Hortense. None of my business, of course, but the thought of him and her together made me feel distinctly grumpy.

CHAPTER NINE

With the banquet less than a week away, Magali is supremely in her element. She sits all morning at her big kitchen table, drawing up sample menus, poring over dog-eared cookery books and food-stained scraps of squared paper bearing recipes in faded ballpoint ink. '*Langouste à la Vanille?*' she murmurs aloud to herself, '*Daube de St-Jacques, poêlée aux endives et citron vert?* Perhaps some baby red mullet would be nice' – she picks her way through a sheaf of scruffy notes – '*et voilà – Filets de petits rougets en écailles de courgettes et à la mousseline de piments.*' She riffles through another clutch of notes. '*Ou bien, Pot-au-feu de pigeon au foie de canard?* Or if I could get hold of some hare – I could do *Râble de lièvre poivré aux choux rouges et aux pommes.*'

Several times she has tried to involve Gaston in her deliberations but, for some reason she cannot fathom, he is sullen and facetious. He watches her with narrowed eyes from his end of the table, smirking as she wades ever deeper into her gastronomic archives.

'Don't you think,' he asks her on the Sunday morning, 'we should maybe find out what this President Bélizon likes to eat? I mean, from what I hear on the street, the man's a card-carryin' cannibal. Maybe you could roast a couple of fat little Indian babies for him.' He senses immediately from her expression that he has overstepped the mark.

'Gaston,' she hisses, picking up a baneful-looking knife and jabbing it in his general direction, 'any more of that *ordure* and I shall fillet your scrawny buttocks for you. Never say such things, even *pour rire.*'

'I thought perhaps, our good friend from the Ministry might have made some suggestion as to the most appropriate comestibles for the occasion.'

'Nobody, but nobody,' she yells at him, 'tells me what I am to cook in my own kitchen. Occasion? What do I care about occasion? I cook what I like to cook and they either eat it or they – or they can *baiser mon cul.*'

He picks up a newspaper and cowers behind it, feigning indifference to her indignation. Devenish strolls in through the back door, red-eyed and limping from his excesses of the previous night.

'What in the name of bleeding charity has happened to all the beer?' he croaks. 'Fridge in the bar's as empty as a leper's dance card.'

'Someone must have drunk it all,' Magali says, with a shrewish glance in her husband's direction. Gaston wearily lays down his paper and yawns.

'Maybe I go fetch some more up from the cellar by and by,' he murmurs, scratching an armpit through the open collar of his shirt.

'I'll give you a hand,' Devenish says, desperate for a drink to muffle the clanging carillon inside his skull.

'No, we can't have that, Monsieur Devenish,' protests Gaston, unfolding himself from his chair like a great mantis. 'You are a guest. It is not proper for you to carry heavy cases of beer up from the cellar and maybe strain your back – give yourself a hernia.' He glares across at Magali. 'That is for me to do all on my own, is it not, *chérie*?' Without looking up, she replies,

'*Your* guest, he may be, but is he still a guest of the Auberge, this is what I would like to know? Is he still a *paying* guest?' At this, Devenish's colour returns and he begins going through his trouser pockets.

'The rent,' he exclaims, 'of course. Don't tell me it's come round again. You really must remind me, Magali. Here, here,' he urges as each pocket yields up its bounty, adding to the growing mound of crumpled greasy bills on the table, 'take what's due out of this.' Magali eyes the money with suspicion.

'You mug someone last night?' she asks.

'In a manner of speaking. Card game. Some young American fathead couldn't give it away fast enough.'

Gaston turns back from the cellar door and asks,

'This American – name of Horowitz?'

'Got it in one. Why, not a friend of yours, I trust?'

'He just moved into number eleven,' Gaston tells him with an upward jerk of his thumb. 'Two doors along from you.'

'Shit.'

While Devenish waits on the veranda for Gaston to bring him a beer, Arden, at Diana's invitation, is taking tea in the annexe. He is ill at ease, though, since the day at the pool and wary now of physical contact with Polly, clumsily rebuffing her more affectionate overtures. He is happy for her to hold his hand and tug his moustache, both of which she does constantly, but when, as today, she attempts to clamber onto his knees he resists, gently but firmly lifting her by the arms and depositing her back on the floor. This she regards as fine sport, and the more he fends her off, the more determined she is to have her way, and she finally ends up on his lap, squirming and giggling, while he, unable to rid his mind of the image of the nakedness beneath the thin cotton frock, grows panicky and breaks into a sweat of self-loathing. Eventually Diana steps in to end the game, full of apologies to him and what Arden takes to be stern imprecations in forest dialect to Polly not to pester the kind English gentleman, but it is too late. He has revisited once more in his mind's eye the ineradicable vision of that bare brown body and still feels its lingering warmth against his loins.

'Were you ever married, Ted?' Diana asks him, holding Polly close to her.

'No, never was, actually,' he replies, struggling both to master and conceal his confusion. 'Engaged once, but that was a long time ago. Water under the bridge, sort of thing.'

'Were you very much in love?'

'Absolutely. Head over heels.'

'But it didn't work out?'

'How do you mean?'

'Forgive me,' she says hastily, 'I have no wish to pry into matters that might cause you distress.'

'No, that's quite all right. Probably do me good to talk about it. So long since. Her name was Rebecca and she worked as a translator, like me. And she was quiet and rather shy – also like me. I suppose you've noticed my wretched lack of self-confidence?'

'You seem a little . . . introspective at times.'

'Well, that's one way of putting it, I suppose – a very kind way, if I might say so. Well, anyway, there we were, two shy people against the world. You know, back-to-back like musketeers, taking on all comers. Between us, we sort of seemed to make one whole person. We made each other feel, somehow, *safe*.'

'So what happened?'

'It was shortly after the time of the handover. I was one of the last out. We'd held the big independence ceremony a couple of months earlier with the flags and military bands and all the pomp and nonsense, but I'd stayed on to supervise the packing up of the library. Things were getting pretty hairy around about then, troops on the street, mobs rioting, cars set on fire, gunshots in the night sort of situation. This was before President Bélizon's big clampdown. Rebecca and I had always planned to set up home on the French side of the island – after we were married, of course – but there was some difficulty with her papers. She didn't have a British passport, and for some reason the French were being uncharacteristically pedantic about visa requirements. The plan was for me to come over first and try to sort something out from this end.

'On my last night I'd promised to take Rebecca out to dinner – finalize arrangements – but when I called for her that evening at her flat I found the door wide open and no sign of her. I sat around for half an hour or so, waiting for her to show up. That's when I noticed that her television set had gone and so had her record player with all her LPs and when I went into the bedroom, all her underwear had been pulled out of the drawers and strewn about the place. Finally a neighbour, an old woman – very cowed and frightened – tapped on the door and told me that some soldiers had taken Rebecca away earlier that afternoon.

'I was frantic. I went straight to the police station, but the place was a madhouse, what with all the civil unrest and general lawlessness. Nobody could tell me anything. The police just laughed in my face when I told them what had happened. "We don't argue with the military," was all they said, "whatever they do is fine by us." As long as I live I shall never forget that odious indifference and the feeling it gave me of total and utter helplessness in the face of it.'

'Oh, my dear God,' Diana whispers. 'Was she involved in politics at all?'

'Not that I know of. We all had our views, of course, but she wasn't a member of a party or anything like that.'

'So what became of her?'

'I don't know. I simply do not know. It's over twenty years now and I have heard nothing from her – nothing *about* her – from that day to this.'

'How absolutely bloody.'

'I mean, her *underwear* – all her lacy little private things, scattered everywhere. By soldiers. It really doesn't bear think-ing about . . .' He falters into silence, his unfocused eyes gazing back into the terrible past and big slow tears begin to roll down his cheeks into his moustache. Diana looks uncomfortably at her feet but Polly stares in open-mouthed astonishment at a sight she has never before seen – a big grown-up white man, crying just like a little baby.

CHAPTER TEN

N ext thing I recall – I think it must have been on the Tuesday morning – was a bit of a sticky meeting with Guitry and Van der Pump about the arrangements for the weekend. Gaston pushed together a couple of tables out on the veranda and the pair of us sat twiddling our thumbs waiting for the bouncing bureaucrat to empty his briefcase and shuffle through his various memos and dockets, while the Afrikaaner kept scanning the frangipani with his little pink eyes for signs of armed insurrection, or maybe greenfly. Finally Guitry dropped something of a minor bombshell on your humble narrator.

'It is agreed, yes, that the President will have the centre room on the upper floor and the rooms either side will be occupied by his guards.'

'Hang about,' I protested, 'what do you mean, "agreed"? Who's agreed this? That's my room in the middle. Do you mean to say that I'm to be turfed out?'

'*Krikt,*' said Van der Pump without taking his eyes off the vegetation, by which I took him to mean, 'correct'. I turned to Gaston, who had the decency to look embarrassed. The long streak of piss had obviously done some devious deal with them on the room rates.

'Well, I must say, I find that a bit much. Why can't he have the corner room? That's been empty for years.'

'It is not considered secure, I regret to say,' said Guitry. 'It will only be for two nights, and I will arrange for my staff to move your things for you. They will be most careful, I can assure you.'

'They'll have to be. I've got all sorts of valuable stuff up there. Antiques and suchlike.'

'We know exactly what you've got up there,' said Van der Pump, with a yawn. 'We've seen it.' Which gave me pause for thought, as you can imagine. I mean a chap's bound to pick up one or two dubious items in the course of a long and colourful life; a Danish magazine or two, the odd tribal carving. Not counting the bathroom cabinet where they'd have learned a lot more than they probably wanted to know about the condition of my piles. Guitry bustled on to the next item.

'The total number of guests attending will be twenty-four, including the President, his team of advisers and a French delegation of eight. You will naturally be attending the banquet in your capacity as . . .' and here I felt his voice took on an unnecessarily sneery tone, '*chef de protocol.*'

'Quite right,' I assured him, 'and I shall be bringing a friend.' At which point Van der Pump swivelled his head round and fixed me with those zombie eyes, and I was all braced for him to say, '*Not krikt,*' but after a second or so he just shrugged and said with a smirk,

'If you've got one, bring one.'

'As to the food,' Guitry went on, and I could see Gaston becoming a bit twitchy, 'we should perhaps consult with Madame Delacroix.'

'No need to consult,' Gaston hastily assured him. 'My wife has already devised a quite exquisite menu – a *menu gourmand* of nine courses – quite *exceptionel* . . .'

Guitry looked down at his notes and said quietly,

'Nevertheless, there are a number of *précautions culinaires* upon which we must insist.'

'*Précautions?*' Gaston was not relishing the prospect of breaking this news to Magali.

'There must be one of our security people in the kitchen at all times while the food is being prepared.' Gaston's face turned a sort of eau de nil.

'Let's cut the crap,' said Van der Pump, except he pronounced it '*crêpe*' which confused the hell out of Gaston. 'I want one of my men checking every single item that goes in and out of that kitchen door – every dish, every ingredient, every herb, every spice. I don't give a shit what's on the menu. My overriding priority is the President's safety.'

'Are you seriously suggesting,' I asked, 'that somebody here in the Auberge might attempt to poison him?'

'Fucking brilliant!' he said, slamming one of those great meaty hands down on the table. 'Did you work that out all by yourself, Mr Devenish? Yes, since you ask, I *am* concerned. The President is concerned, so I am concerned. His concerns, in short, are my concerns. So I'll tell you something else which is going to happen, if it's all right by you – merely as a precaution, you understand. When each of those – what was it? – nine courses is in the kitchen, ready to be served, my man will choose one of the twenty-four plates at random to be presented to the President. Then the only way someone could be sure of getting him is to poison the whole lot of you.' Gaston looked like a man who's just heard his dog's been run over.

Guitry rambled on through his interminable agenda of items, none of which stuck in my mind but, to be honest, my attention had begun to wander a bit by this point. Just as he was wittering on about motorcycle escorts, Ted hove in view at the end of the veranda. He took one look at the group of us and turned tail but before he could make his escape, Van der Pump was up and on him like a fer-de-lance.

'Mr Arden, is it not?' he said, wrapping an arm round Ted's shoulders and steering him back towards the assembled company. 'Join us. We have a small favour to ask of you.' Ted stood there blinking while he was introduced to Guitry. The little frog struggled for a moment, trying to remember what it was he was supposed to ask Ted, and then it came to him.

'Mr Arden,' he said. 'It is a pleasure to meet you. You were an interpreter, I understand, in the old colonial days.'

'No, I was a translator. I translated documents.'

'Nonetheless, you do speak French, I believe?'

'Yes, I do.'

'Then perhaps I might prevail upon you, on the night of the banquet, to make your own small contribution towards international understanding . . .'

'I shall not be attending the banquet,' Ted announced. Guitry seemed nonplussed by this and turned to Van der Pump for help. The South African responded with a brisk little shake of his head.

'But of course you will be attending,' Guitry insisted. 'You are invited. You will be the guest of the French government.'

'I'm sorry,' Ted said, 'but I cannot possibly attend. I have

73

other things to do on the night in question. Matters to attend to.'

'Mr Arden,' Van der Pump said, with an unmistakable note of exasperation in his voice, 'what "matters" are you referring to? Perhaps something touching on the problem of your residency status here in France?'

'What are you talking about? There is no problem with my residency status – absolutely none . . .' Ted started to protest and then he twigged. 'My residency status?' he mumbled, and then, 'What exactly is it you want me to do?' Guitry beamed at him.

'I would be obliged, Mr Arden, if you would allow yourself to be seated among the members of the French delegation in order to translate any of President Bélizon's utterances which may not be clear to them. Because this is an "informal" occasion, we have dispensed with most of the official interpreters, but you, as a fellow guest at the Auberge, will be perfectly placed to assist the flow of conversation.'

'I will do what I can,' Ted said glumly.

'The troops will be moving into position early tomorrow morning,' Guitry resumed. 'They will not be deployed within the grounds of the Auberge, but they will stand guard at the gates and patrol the perimeter night and day; they will also mount surveillance from the hills above. They will have their own electricity generators and their own field rations but we shall need to supply them with water. Can that be arranged?'

'I suppose that'll need to be tested for poison as well,' I said, by way of a joke.

'Bloody good point,' said Van der Pump.

CHAPTER ELEVEN

Gaston's early morning dreams are put to flight by a juddering, mechanical throb which insinuates itself into his darkened bedroom, growing louder by the minute until the whole fabric of the building begins to shake, sending his chipped toothmug skittering across the marble surface of the washstand until it topples from the edge and smashes on the floor. With an oath he untangles himself from the damp coils of his sheets, hobbles over to the window and flings wide the shutters.

Just beyond the Auberge gateposts a monstrous khaki half-track – an armoured car with its gun turret shrouded in a dusty tarpaulin – is fitfully coughing out plumes of foul black smoke in its struggle to negotiate the narrow bend in the road up into the hills. Van der Pump stands beside the vehicle, screeching abuse at the unseen driver within, slashing at the windshield slit with his swagger stick. Seven or eight uniformed men are positioned to the rear, their backs against the rusted panelling as they sweat and strain to swivel the intransigent behemoth into position. After fifteen deafening minutes, the thing inches round and roars away up the road, the metal tracks squealing as they struggle to gain traction on the fierce and stony incline. With his legionnaire's critical eye, Gaston notes the scruffy turnout of the troops, the missing buttons, the grubby brass, and he murmurs to himself,

'*Bande de macaques.*'

As the sound of the vehicle fades into the echoing hills, Gaston painstakingly gathers up the pieces of broken crockery and makes his way downstairs. In the dining room he finds Horowitz sharing a table with the woman, the pair of them deep in hushed conversation. Gaston bestows a distant nod upon them as he passes through.

In the kitchen Magali sulks, still unreconciled to the prospect of having to accommodate strangers within her hallowed walls for the banquet preparations. She is once more listening to her treasured Brassens tape, but even the familiar scurrilous verse about him catching crabs from *Madame la Marquise* fails to bring a smile to her lips. As Gaston appears, she glares at him and asks,

'So what was all that outside? Felt like some kind of earthquake back here.'

Gaston helps himself to a bowl of coffee and waves his hand airily in the direction of the mountains.

'*Bande de Zouaves* with an armoured car.' He has to shout to make himself heard over the music.

'What, the army, you mean?'

'Some riffraff from across the border, I shouldn't wonder – some kind of presidential guard, maybe. They are not French, that's for certain sure, and why should the government allow a bunch of armed men from some private foreign army to drive a fucking great armoured car through a *département* of France? You want to know what I think?'

Magali shrugs and begins kneading the dough for the evening's bread.

'What you think?'

'I tell you what I think. I think the security for this visit is being put into the hands of Van der Pump and his shabby little *troupe* because maybe it suits the French authorities to wash their hands of this business. Maybe they know that something is bound to go wrong and they don't want to get the blame.'

This thought troubles him, because in his experience any blame that is going around tends to attach itself like a leech to Gaston Delacroix.

'And what about the American?' he goes on. 'How come he shows up right at this particular moment in time? This is bad news, take it from me. This part of the world, Americans are bad news, always up to something, plotting and making mischief. Playing politics like they might be playing checkers. What you bet you he's CIA or something?'

'You're crazy. He's well too fat to be CIA.'

'Yeah? Well maybe they recruit the odd fat one, just to put you off the trail. You ever think of that?'

Devenish staggers into the room, wagging his head from side to side and banging his hand against one temple like a swimmer trying to rid his ears of water.

'What in the name of all the holy prophets is going on round here? Half the bloody ceiling's just come down on me. Plaster all over the shop.'

'Troop movements,' Gaston tells him.

'Sodding bastards,' Devenish mutters, ruffling his hair and releasing a cloud of white dust.

'What you think this Horowitz up to?' Magali calls across. 'Gaston reckon he with the CIA. What you reckon?'

'Not a chance. Take it from a man who's played cards with him. He's thick as pigshit and only a touch more fragrant. That's how you can spot the boys from Langley, in my experience – you can smell 'em a mile away. Much too heavy-handed with the toiletries. No, that chubby little chappie is exactly what he seems – a spoilt rich moron.'

'Well, I reckon there's something a bit dubious about him,'

says Gaston. 'He and that woman thick as thieves when I come through the breakfast room by and by.'

'Were they, indeed?' asks the disgruntled Devenish, brushing the last of the plaster dust from his scalp. 'I can see I shall have to step in there a bit lively.'

When he reaches the dining room, though, Horowitz has disappeared and Diana sits motionless, gazing out into the gardens, where Polly is studiously turning cartwheels on the dewy lawn. He flops down beside her, uncomfortably aware of the damply lingering warmth left in the chair by the recently departed Horowitz. As she turns, smiling, to face him, he says,

'Good morning, ma'am, I trust you were not roused too rudely from your slumbers this morning. Some military goings-on, by all accounts.'

'Not at all, Mr Devenish. I was up before sunrise. The dawn light on the mountains was quite superb this morning.'

'Wonderful sight, wonderful sight. No finer spot on the face of the earth.'

'Every prospect pleases, eh?'

'And only man is vile, what?'

'Is that really what you feel?' she asks. 'Do you not miss your home country at all? I assume you are from England, originally.'

81

'Never give it a second's thought, to tell you the truth. Way I see it, England is something to carry around with you. It's a wonderful place in theory, but it's not somewhere you want to go back to. Spoils the illusion completely. Went over to London a few years ago – some legal business – place was absolutely filthy. Downtrodden surly faces wherever you looked, beggars in cardboard boxes on every street corner. Travelled on the underground once. Everything stank of urine.'

'But, surely, the English countryside . . . ?'

'Oh, it's all fine and dandy on a perfect summer's day, with a decent game of cricket on the green and the sound of skylarks overhead, but how many of those do you get in the course of a year? No, it's mostly as drab and boring as a wet breeze block. You ever go back?'

'I have never been to England, alas. I was born out here and so I have no real feeling for the country, other than from the stories I was told as a girl. But I have always felt there is something rather special about being English.'

'Ah, well, now you're talking. Being English is a damn fine thing, I grant you that, and nobody can take it away from you. Civilized values, live and let live, proper respect for tradition and all that. It's just the country itself that's gone down the toilet, from what I can tell.'

Outside, Arden wanders into view and is immediately roped into a game of hide-and-seek with Polly. Devenish watches the two of them playing for a while and remarks,

'Look at him out there, frisking about like a two-year-old. Your little . . .' He finds himself forming the phrase 'jungle bunny' but something about the look in her eye makes him swallow the words.

'Polly,' she prompts. 'My little Polly.'

'Exactly,' he agrees, nodding vigorously. 'Your little Polly has certainly managed to bring Ted Arden out of his shell. No two ways about it.'

Arden joins them, out of breath from his exertions among the shrubs. He hovers by their table, mopping his red face with a large linen handkerchief and Devenish says, more jauntily than he feels,

'We were just talking about what a fine thing it is to be English.'

'Really?' Arden inquires, folding the handkerchief tidily away into his top jacket pocket. 'In what sense?'

Devenish is nonplussed.

'Goes without saying, old man, surely. Most civilized nation on earth. Only country worth fighting for.'

'Why the devil should I have to fight for England? Why on earth should I want to?'

83

'But it's your native land, man. Where you were born. You'd have to fight for the land of your birth, if it came to the crunch.'

'That's preposterous,' Arden says. 'Why should you have to fight for a country just because you were born there? You've got to be born somewhere. Does that mean you're duty bound to fight for that place, no matter what you happen to believe?'

'Bravo, Edward,' Diana tells him and Devenish sniffs loudly, tossing his head in exasperation at this unexpected alliance against him.

'Never had you marked down for some namby-pamby pacifist, Ted,' he murmurs. 'Always thought you were made of sterner stuff.'

'It's not pacifism,' Arden tells him stiffly. 'I'm as ready to fight as the next man. But I believe one should fight for a principle, not some accident of birth.'

'Like the Nazis, you mean?' Devenish sneers. 'Serving some psychopath's crackpot vision of what the world should be like?'

'I don't mean a political cause,' Arden persists. 'I mean a private principle. One should be prepared to fight to defend one's own property and to protect one's family. I cannot see the merit of going to war in furtherance of an abstract idea.'

'Besides which,' Diana adds, 'I think you'll find the majority of German troops were persuaded they were fighting for the Fatherland, rather than for the Nazi ideal. It may not be easy, Mr Devenish, to find men who are prepared to lay down their lives for their country, but it's a damn sight harder to find men willing to die for their politicians.'

Devenish snorts and gets to his feet.

'Well, I can't sit around here all day,' he announces, 'Alphonse is due in tomorrow and there's bugger all been done, as far as I can see.'

When he has gone, Diana asks Arden,

'Were you ever in the Forces?'

'National Service. We were the last intake. I spent two years in the Intelligence Corps. Black Forest. Ended up as a major. No fighting involved, of course.'

'You were conscripted?'

'Yes. Never really felt like a soldier. More like a civilian in uniform.'

'But then, conscripts are all civilians until they're called up. I always think it curious how we talk about civilian casualties in wartime, because of course if you've been conscripted, you have no choice. It has often occurred to me that many of the soldiers who died in the two world wars – on both sides – were civilian casualties.'

'Will you be attending the banquet?'

'I rather think I shall. That funny little man Guitry has invited me. I told him that I might represent something of an embarrassment to the President, but he seemed to think that a little embarrassment would be no bad thing on this occasion. I'm afraid the politics here run very deep and very murky.'

'What are they trying to achieve, do you think? Jack thinks it's something to do with bauxite.'

'Bauxite?' she smiles gently. 'Is that what they're putting out? No, I think you'll find it has a lot more to do with Bélizon's dynastic ambitions and the fragile state of his health.'

'Is he not well? There's been nothing in the papers.'

'He needs two things from the French. He needs money and he needs surgery. Without treatment, he fears that he will die before he can consolidate his son's position as President-in-Waiting and without the money to pay the army, his son will never be able to keep them loyal.'

'So what do the French get out of this?'

'That's where it gets murky. The French seem to think that the continuation of the Bélizon line would be no bad thing, or rather that it would be a better thing than the alternative.'

'Which is?'

'There are a number of . . . factions, you might call them

86

– groups of separatist fanatics – who believe that the whole island should be united. That the French have no right to be here and direct military action could drive them out.'

'But that's absurd. How could they possibly hope to intimidate the French? Good God, there's a Nato naval base down there.' He gestures towards the coast. 'There are warships and helicopters and stuff. The British and the Americans would bomb them back to the forest.'

'I don't think it would be that kind of a war and I suspect the Americans may be pursuing their own agenda here. Washington could have its reasons for destabilizing the Bélizon regime. And the separatists, you see, are not just on one side of the border. The whole thing could get very bloody indeed if the factions over there seize control of the military and start shipping *plastique* and AK-74s to their comrades over here.'

'But surely, they couldn't sustain the kind of terrorist action that would drive the French off the island?'

'Ever heard of a place called "Dien Bien Phu"?'

'And that's what they're afraid of?'

'That's what we should all be afraid of.'

'So the French are propping up this monster, simply to keep the separatists in line. They're prepared to put up the cash to keep this repugnant regime in place, simply for fear of something worse. What kind of morality is that, for God's sake?'

'It's not morality, Ted, it's enlightened self-interest. In other words, politics.'

He stares out across the gardens, where Polly has resumed her gymnastics, and says quietly,

'Well, I think it stinks.'

CHAPTER TWELVE

To tell you the truth, as the week wore on, Ted Arden began to get more than somewhat up my nose. Not only was he forever traipsing around after Diana and her little piccaninny, queering the pitch good and proper for yours truly, but the two of them had taken to voicing some damn peculiar political opinions. And if there's one thing you learn when you're an expat, living as the guest of a foreign power, it's to keep your nose out of their politics.

The French in particular are very touchy on that score, not that anybody understands their politics, mind you. Someone – I think it was that bad-tempered television historian who used to wear the bow ties – said that French politics was like a game of musical chairs, except they never took a chair away. It was all backhanders and corruption, as far as he could make out. In England it's a mystery why anyone goes into politics. Thankless bloody task. But in France, you go into politics to get your hand in the till. Everybody knows that, but as I say, it's not something you go around shouting about.

But I digress. Friday morning just after sunup Gaston and I were up on the roof of the Auberge, watching bleary-eyed as the presidential yacht dropped anchor in the bay. Sodding great thing, cost twice the country's annual welfare budget, or so the story goes. Sinister-looking bloody craft, too – stainless steel, by the looks of it – twin funnels right at the back with a helicopter pad slung between them. Gaston was peering through his old Foreign Legion binoculars, but there was bugger all to see except a bunch of matelots clambering about at the sharp end.

'What time's he due up here?' I asked.

'Some time this afternoon is what they tell me,' and he swung his glasses round to look up the hill at Van der Pump's merry men, who were just beginning to stumble out of their tents in their khaki undershorts, yawning and spitting and scratching their arses in the sunlight. '*Bande de crétins*,' was all he said. We climbed down through the trapdoor and made our way back along the mansard floor, bent double under the low roof and trying not to kick up the layers of sour dust, which must have been accumulating there since the time of Napoleon.

Back in the kitchen the atmosphere was thicker than cassoulet. Magali's own reign of terror had begun. Although the big feast wasn't until the Saturday night, she was already in a high old state. She'd rounded up her usual bunch of teenage layabouts from the town and she was determined to drill them into shape, trying to transform a band of reluctant halfwits into a *brigade* of semi-competent *plongeurs*, commis waiters, and sous-chefs – all in twenty-four hours. Her most persuasive teaching aid was a heavy copper ladle which she administered at unpredictable intervals to one or other of her pupil's skulls. Made a noise like a Chinese gong.

Gaston and I beat a strategic retreat to the veranda for coffee and a sharpener. Best way to set you up for the day, in my humble opinion. Bowl of coffee, black as sin with a shot of cognac in it. Can't understand all this 'over the yardarm' business. Why shouldn't a chap take a snifter at seven o'clock in the morning, if he feels so inclined? Way I see it, it's always sundown somewhere in the world and the Courvoisier doesn't know what time it is. Gaston had to be a bit more circumspect, of course, on account of his old woman giving him big stick if she caught him tucking into the falling-down water before breakfast, but he kept a bottle stashed away under a loose plank in the veranda decking so he wouldn't have to open up the bar and rattle her cage.

It must have been about quarter to eight, just when the second snort of hot brandy fumes was well and truly fumigating the old frontal lobes, when who should toddle out in his baggy

Bermudas but young Horowitz, already sweating like a warm Cheddar and slapping the mosquitoes from his lardy legs.

'Is this true, what I hear?' he asked us.

'Er . . . can you give us a bit more of a clue?' I said.

'You guys are having a banquet here Saturday night for Bélizon?'

'We guys?' Gaston cackled. 'Not we guys. The French government is holding a formal state dinner for our esteemed neighbour. I shall be pouring the drinks.'

'No shit. Do you think I could get an interview with him?'

'Why would you want to interview him?' asked Gaston, suddenly suspicious.

'Alphonse Bélizon – are you kidding? Do you have any idea what an interview with him would be worth? Jeez, it could make the *Times*, maybe even the *New Yorker*. I could be a made man.'

'Pardon my asking,' I said, 'but am I to understand that you are some sort of newspaper scribe?'

'Well, it's not my major study, but I've done some pretty neat stuff for the campus magazine and, hell, this is the chance of a lifetime – this is a whole future career in journalism just walking right up and saying, "Take me, I'm yours".'

As luck would have it, Van der Pump stuck his ugly mug

round the far end of the veranda at this point, and I said to Horowitz, 'There's your man. Ask him.' The young fathead lolloped up to the glowering Boer and said,

'Pardon me, sir, but do you think President Bélizon would grant me the honour of a personal interview?'

Van der Pump whipped off his sunglasses and looked him up and down like he was trying to decide which limb to wrench off first, and then grinned. He patted the poor little sod gently on the cheek and walked on with a slow shake of his head. He passed Gaston and me without breaking stride and all he said was,

'Where d'you find Miss Piggy?'

Undeterred, Horowitz sidled back to join us, remarkably chipper, I thought, under the circumstances.

'So when do you guys figure would be the best time to approach him?' he asked.

'Depends what time you fancy getting your arms broken,' I told him. 'They're not just *playing* soldiers, you know. He's an evil bastard, that Van der Pump. I wouldn't like to get on the wrong side of him – not that I've caught sight of a *right* side so far.'

'Shit, they can't touch me, I'm an American citizen.'

And the young ass waddled off to get himself some breakfast. Gaston poured us both another snifter and we sat for a while in companionable contemplation of the landscape until he suddenly asked,

'You ever kill anyone, Jack Devenish?'

'No, can't say that I ever did. Came close to it a couple of times, of course. My line of work, hard to avoid. What about you?'

'Two or three, maybe. But that was when I was with *la Légion*.'

'Why do you ask? You got someone in mind?'

'No, no, no,' he protested, spluttering into his coffee bowl. 'I was just watching Van der Pump, and I was thinking to myself, such a man would kill without hesitation or regret. Do you not think so?'

'No question about it, my old son. No doubt whatsoever.'

'Only I was saying to Magali that maybe there's something not right about this whole setup.' He was talking in barely a whisper by now. 'How come our own police aren't providing the *sécurité* for this president? Why are they leaving it up to a *bande de voyous* like this mob? Maybe they *want* something to happen to the old bastard. And why does that woman turn up right now?'

'You're not suggesting she's some sort of assassin, are you? You're getting paranoid in your old age, Gaston. First you think that young fool, Horowitz, is CIA and now you're convinced the fair Diana is some kind of contract killer. You want to get a grip on yourself, old man. You're getting as bad as Van der Pump. Next thing you'll be telling me that your old lady's going to be slipping rat poison into the President's bedtime cocoa.'

'No, but,' he went on, apparently in deadly earnest, 'she is mixed up in some pretty dangerous politics.'

'Who, Magali?'

'No, no – the other one. Madame Lacombe. You know her husband disappeared. Or rather I should say he was *made* to disappear. There was much talk when it happened about a plot, a coup d'état and he was mixed up in it somehow. The two of them were.'

'A plot against who?'

'Bélizon.'

'Holy Mother of God.'

Later that morning I found myself bending the old elbow at the bar of the *Macaque Agile*, waiting for Hortense to show up. She wanted me to help her choose a ball gown or some such nonsense for the big occasion, and I had a shrewd idea who'd be expected to pick up the tab. There was no sign of Alfie, and the barman told me they'd commandeered his Hispano-Suiza for the official presidential motorcade up to the Auberge. I was just trickling water into my second Ricard, when there was an almighty kerfuffle outside, much hollering and screeching and then a couple of loud bangs.

We all shambled over to the windows for a look-see and there was the old Black Maria – the *panier à salade* – with half a dozen riot police bundling a pair of scruffy herberts into the back, and laying into them with their billy clubs – usual sort of carry-on. One of the prisoners was clinging on like grim death to the back doorframe to stop himself being dragged inside but a *flic* stomped on his fingers and you could hear the scream through the plate glass *vitrine*. Only unusual thing was the couple of dodgy-looking thugs leaning against a jeep parked across the road who I took to be GIGN counterterrorist boys. At any rate, they were all done up in flak jackets with grenade throwers tucked under their arms.

The whole business was done and dusted in two shakes of a rat's willy, and they all roared off, giving it plenty of klaxon and leaving nothing behind but a smashed, bloodstained placard in the gutter which said something about Bélizon and political prisoners. You've got to hand it to the French; when it comes to dealing with protesters and similar riffraff, they don't muck about. Rough justice, you might call it, but it does keep the streets nice and tidy. We all exchanged shrugs and drifted back to the bar. Nobody said anything. Nobody ever did.

Hortense showed up half an hour late, by which time I was a trifle poodled, what with the dawn cognac and three or four Ricards. This was just as well, because as she dragged me round the posh frock shops of the *quartier*, trying on this and that, and we gradually accumulated a collection of shiny carrier bags, I hardly felt a thing. Mind you, it did occur to me that I might have to organize another card game with Horowitz to fund this little shopping expedition. Still, Hortense was having a whale of a time and that's all that mattered, as far as I was concerned. I wasn't planning to settle down and raise a family with her, but she was good enough company while it lasted.

We sat out on the terrace of one of those big hotels on the esplanade and she insisted on ordering a plate of langoustines and a bottle of Crystal, although I was damn sure by this time that my credit card would be starting to glow in the dark. We clinked glasses, and she said,

'Do you know why we do that?'

'Do what?'

'Chink-chink.'

'Never really thought about it.'

'It's because you can appreciate God's good wine with all yo' other senses, 'cepting your ears. You can see it and smell it and feel it and taste it, but you can't hear it. So – chink-chink.'

'Well I never,' I said. She got to work on the shellfish, cracking the claws open with those huge white gnashers of hers and swilling the bubbly round her gums after each mouthful.

'You hear anything about any trouble brewing in town?' I asked her.

'Trouble 'bout what?' She stopped eating and mopped her chin with her napkin.

'About the presidential visit. Just before you got to the bar, the RAID boys grabbed a couple of protesters off the street.'

'I'm hearing nothing 'bout no trouble.' She chuckled. 'Why, you think maybe you in some danger?'

'Had occurred to me. Someone's certainly expecting trouble. It's crawling with troops back at the Auberge. Some heavyweight ironmongery up there.'

'So, they looking after your precious ass. Prob'ly safest place to be on the whole island, up there with uncle Alphonse. Don't you worry 'bout a thing.'

'You ever been mixed up in the politics here at all?'

'I got more sense.' She polished off the seafood and I walked her back to the flat. She turned to me at the door with a little crooked grin on her face and said,

'You want a quickie? Say thanks for the frock and all?' And

although I was too pissed to do it, I wasn't too pissed to know, so I told her,

'Save it for next time.'

'I'll keep practising.'

On the way back, there were motorcycle police with walkie-talkies at every intersection and when I reached the Auberge, a couple of Van der Pump's goons with sub-machine-guns were posted either side of the entrance. Gaston was on the front step, hopping from foot to foot dressed in his Sunday best, his face scraped and raw from its recent encounter with the unfamiliar razor. He was wearing a sort of yellow linen suit that looked like a much larger man had been sleeping in it. As I arrived, Guitry came bustling out from behind him, tapping his wristwatch, and saying,

'*Une heure, pas plus.*' Gaston rolled his eyes to the heavens and straightened his stringy tie. Never seen a chap looking so discomfited. I gave Guitry a perfunctory nod and went up to my room for a spot of shut-eye.

CHAPTER THIRTEEN

There are six motorcycle outriders, and the thrum and rumble of their engines unrolls before them, burbling back and forth between the high buildings in the narrow town streets. They are followed by the official vehicles of the *département* – two venerable black Citroën DS19s, veterans of the De Gaulle years and polished to a glassy lustre – which have been nursed and cajoled into life for this historic occasion. In their wake, the mighty Hispano-Suiza, inexpertly driven by the monocular Alfred Petrosian, amateur barkeeper and professional smuggler, weaves its way erratically up into the hills, bearing the august personage of Alphonse Bélizon. Behind this comes a flat-bed truck, laden with baggage followed by two jeeps crammed with heavily armed militia.

Van der Pump, in the full dress uniform of some unidentifiable paramilitary force, is clearly visible in the front passenger seat of the limousine, both hands firmly gripping the dashboard, but the President himself is tucked so far back into the upholstered interior that only one arm can be seen through the side window, the hand clinging to a chubby red silken rope. It is a remarkably small hand, brown and bony, like something preserved in a sarcophagus, or a bog. It does not wave, this hand, or show any sign of animation, other than to sway gently with the motion of the car.

The route is not thronged with cheering sightseers. Out in the countryside the occasional *paysan* pauses in his labours to rest on his mattock and peer incuriously at the motorcade as it rumbles past. A woman, weighed down with shopping baskets, spits on the ground, and stands glaring after the disappearing procession until its image fragments and fades in the rippling, dusty heat haze. Inside the giant limousine, behind the glass partition, the air is thick and stifling, but Bélizon keeps the windows tightly closed. He does not perspire. His tiny, shrivelled body has lost too much fat for him to suffer from the heat. The cancer, which at one time threatened to liquefy his left kidney and carry him off in paroxysmal agony, is still in remission, as a result of the gruelling course of radical surgery and chemotherapy carried out secretly two years before in a Harley Street clinic. But the treatment has left him debilitated and has exacerbated a weakness in his heart. He needs another operation, a coronary bypass, but he can no longer risk returning to England. Not after all that wretched business with Pinochet. No, he knows that the British are no longer to be trusted. The French he feels more comfortable about. It is true, of course, they are also members of that big European club, but the French are quite happy to ignore the club rules when it suits them. He feels confident with the French, he feels safe. He knows they will do a deal.

The trouble is, he reflects, these days you can't really trust anybody completely. Not even your own flesh and blood. Look at that boy of his, Alphonse Junior. Boy? Forty-seven years old and growing ever more impatient for power. But the lad is soft and stupid, with cranky liberal notions of human rights and other such twaddle. His only chance is the army, and the army has no respect for him. As president, the only thing Bélizon can do for his son and heir is to hang on, to do a deal, to get some hard currency into the treasury. That would command respect. Otherwise there can be no hope for the young idiot. Was there a plot? Van der Pump had told him weeks ago that Junior was making covert approaches to some of the generals, but was there any truth in it? He knows from long experience that Van der Pump is a devious conniving bastard with his own Byzantine agenda.

Blood, dammit. You couldn't just walk away from it. The boy is seed of his loins, family. And stupid family is still family, when all is said and done. The generals are another matter. One or two of them could disappear easily, but there again he would have to tread carefully. He just wishes to God that he did not have to leave the country at this time. While the cat is away, the rats can do whatever they damn well please. Well, it can't be helped. It's either die tomorrow or die the day after. No choice. Ask any condemned man.

As the motorcade arrives at the Auberge and before the giant limousine comes to rest, Van der Pump jumps down and opens the President's door. Three bulky black men in pale blue gabardine suits squeeze themselves out of the Citroëns and take up a prearranged protective formation between the car and the porch. They all have white pork-pie hats perched on their closely cropped heads and identical wraparound sunglasses. Beneath the taut fabric of their jackets there is an almost cubic solidity to their musculature. Gaston watches in disgust from the entrance. '*Quelle pantomime!*' he mutters to himself.

For almost a minute, nobody moves. Then slowly, laboriously, Bélizon emerges from the car, feeling for the ground with a silver-topped ebony cane and leaning heavily on Van der Pump's arm as he steps down from the high running board. The President is barely five feet tall, and wears an olive, medal-ribboned uniform, the trousers of which bear a wide red stripe, terminating incongruously at ground level over a pair of two-tone wing-tips in cream canvas and crocodile hide.

His wispy hair is a curious orange colour and hangs in long skeins about his head, waving in the breeze like the tentacles of some exotic jellyfish, until Van der Pump reaches into the car and passes him a peaked cap, encrusted with gold braid. He covers his head and squints unsmilingly about him, his rheumy, yellow-rimmed eyes taking in the crumbling villa, the armoured car high on the hill behind, and the jaunty figure of Guitry as that diminutive bureaucrat skips forward, hand outstretched, to welcome his guest to France on behalf of the *République*. Bélizon proffers three shrunken fingers, which Guitry grasps cautiously, as though fearful of having them come away in his hand, and the old man walks on into the Auberge, pausing for a brief moment on the threshold to cast a suspicious glance into Gaston's face, before hobbling forward into the cool, dark interior of the hall.

There, against the side wall, he finds a hard wooden bench onto which he carefully lowers his wasted frame and waits for his eyes to adjust to the musty gloom. He sits there, wheezing quietly as the minutes pass, rapping the ferrule of his stick rhythmically on the flagstones. Two of the body-guards, escorted by Gaston, climb the stairs to check out the presidential quarters while, piece by piece, the presidential luggage is carried in, forming an aromatic wall of polished brown leather beside him. Finally he removes the cap, clears his throat and remarks, in soft, clear tones,

'They tell me the food here is very good.' The accent embodies all the upper-middle-class languor of the post-war British cinema.

'The best on the island, *Monsieur le Président*,' Gaston tells him with an obsequious little bow. Bélizon nods.

'Who was that driver?' he asks after a pause. 'Who in God's name was that maniac of a driver?' Nobody answers and he looks around him once more, humming quietly to himself. He hauls himself shakily to his feet and walks over to examine some imperfection on the wall opposite. He raps sharply on it with the tip of his cane, dislodging a chunk of plaster.

'What a dump,' he sighs eventually. 'What a shit hole. What an absolute fucking awful shit hole of a dump.'

CHAPTER FOURTEEN

Woken by the noise of motorbikes, I tottered across the landing into one of the empty front bedrooms to watch the arrival of the great man. Bound to say, he did not resemble a well bunny. Tiny, shrivelled creature, looked like he was made of old banana skins. Seemed none too steady on his stalks, either, though that could have been Alfie's driving. Even Van der Pump, I was chuffed to note, was looking a bit queasy after the ride up the mountain. But it was hard to believe that here was one of the great villains of the twentieth century, one of the most evil tyrants on the face of the planet, as Ted would have it. Mind you, I hadn't at this point had the honour of speaking to the man. It wasn't till later on that same evening I came to see that maybe old Ted had a point.

It took them most of the afternoon to get him settled into my old quarters, with those bullyboys of his crashing up and down stairs with the cabin trunks and what have you. All Louis Vuitton, mind you – no rubbish. I kept to my room, out of harm's way, keeping the impending hangover at arm's length with regular snorts out of the flask, until just before sunset when I ventured forth in search of a snack. I was sort of hoping Magali would fix me up with a *croque-monsieur* or something. Fat chance. The kitchen was like something out of Dante's Inferno, so choked with steam and smoke you couldn't see from one side to the other and Magali in a right flap, shrieking like a banshee at anything that moved, and several things that didn't. As I came through the door, I swear to God I saw her punch a big catfish right in the mouth. Could have been some hush-hush part of the recipe, I suppose, but I reckon she just didn't like the way it was looking at her.

I ducked out through the back way into the cool of the evening and who should I encounter but Gaston and Alfie, side by side with their feet up on the balustrade, knocking back the rum punches.

'Hey, Jack, where are you being all day?' Alfie called out, waving me across to join them. 'You miss the big parade.'

'How's business Alfred?' I asked him. 'They paying you for this driving job?'

'Shit, no. This I am doing as a favour to the gov'ment. They do me a favour, I do them one.'

'What favour they do you, Alfie?' Gaston asked. 'Not throwin' you in the poky?'

'Could be part of it,' he admitted. 'Me and the gov'ment

are not always seeing strictly eye to eye on the subject of personal taxation.' He flipped his black eyepatch up onto his forehead and scratched at the scarred socket. 'We have the ongoing dialogue, like it might be.'

I wandered through to the bar, helped myself to a beer and returned to join the party.

'So what did you make of our illustrious guest?' I asked Alfie. 'Did he tip you when you dropped him off?'

'Does not say a word the whole way up. Maybe is grunting a bit from time to time. That big South African is telling me there is something wrong with the old boy's ticker.'

'There something wrong with *everybody's* ticker after a ride with you, Alfie,' said Gaston. Alfie fixed him with his one good eye and grinned.

'You saying I am a dangerous driver or something?'

'You saying the anaconda a dangerous snake?'

Dinner that night was to be a perfunctory sort of affair, Gaston explained, but this was on account of all the preparations being made in the kitchen for the next day's banquet. Bélizon, apparently exhausted by the journey, was having a tray taken up to his room. Gaston built another brace of rum punches for him and Alfie and we were all about to settle in for a nice, quiet session when one of the bodyguards came tumbling out through the kitchen door, holding his hands over his head while Magali laid into him with that big copper ladle. She was screaming a blue streak at him in French, and although I didn't follow every word, Gaston was wincing a fair bit, so I imagine it was pretty ripe material. He hopped up and tried to get between them, although I got the impression it was not Magali he thought was in need of protection. He eventually took the ladle away from her and said,

'Hey, hey, woman. What's the big problem here?'

'*Voleur!*' she hissed at the big black feller. 'Thieving bastard! You want rum, you pay for rum.'

'Lady,' protested the poor chap, his eyes full of panic, 'I have to taste *everythin*' – it's my job.'

'Taste? Taste?' she yelled. 'You need to taste best part of a bottle of me finest Martinique vintage rum? What you think – maybe I put the poison just in the bottom part?' They stood glowering at each other for a while, Magali with her hands on her hips and the bodyguard breathing heavily and holding his mitts protectively out in front of him, watching for her next move.

'This true, what she say?' Gaston asked.

'Maybe I take a coupla drinks,' the chap admitted with a shrug, 'but, shit, man, I never drink no whole bottle. No way.'

'What's your name?'

'Winston.'

'I tell you what, Winston, my man,' said Gaston, draping a sinewy arm round the man's shoulders. 'You want a drink? You have a drink with us.'

The chap shook his head sadly and said,

'I have to go back to the kitchen,' and then hastily to Magali, 'I don't *want* to be in there, lady – I *have* to be. Like I tell you, it's my job.' Gaston handed the ladle over to Magali and the bodyguard followed her nervously back into the kitchen.

'Hot shit!' said Alfie. 'That's one scary woman. You ever play around, Gaston? You maybe get a little bit of pussy on the side?'

'Not me.' Gaston shuddered and shook his head like a terrier with a rat.

'That maybe explains how come you are living so long, I think,' said Alfie.

The meal was well up to scratch that night, in spite of Gaston's words of caution. It was some kind of fragrant Cajun fish broth, I remember, followed by a fiery goat curry, hot enough to numb your lips and blast the cobwebs out of your sinuses. There were only a handful of us in the dining room. Diana and the moppet shared a table with Horowitz; Ted made up a threesome with Alfie and me. Only one of the goons was in evidence, sat on his own at a corner table,

111

scowling at the lot of us with his shades perched on top of his fuzzy thatch. After a first-rate papaya *crème brûlée*, the whole bunch of us – except for the goon – made our way out to the veranda for coffee and a nightcap under the stars. We formed a rough circle round a couple of tables and the chaps lit up cigars. Gaston did the honours with the liqueur chariot and the world seemed a pretty damned tolerable place, all things considered. It was right about then that Bélizon put in an appearance, and things began to take a distinct turn for the peculiar.

He stood there in the doorway, wearing Doc Marten boots, black cotton trousers and a cornflower blue Hawaiian shirt, printed with pink flamingos and green palm trees. Clipped into the top pocket he had one of those big black Montblanc fountain pens. He smiled at us and said, with a gracious flourish of his crabby little hand,

'Do please continue, ladies and gentlemen. No need to stand on ceremony, I assure you.' And d'you know something? He sounded for all the world like Trevor Howard in *Brief Encounter*. Of course, soon as he said that, all the blokes sprang to their feet and stood around looking foolish until Ted, of all people, said,

'*Monsieur le Président*, would you care to join us?' I couldn't have been more astonished if he'd dropped his

112

trousers and sung a selection from *The Mikado*. Bélizon smiled and nodded, picking his way through the chairs with the help of his cane and the arm of a bodyguard who had followed him out. Ted ushered the great man to his own chair and pulled up a stool for himself, and when we were all settled again it was Bélizon who broke the silence by asking Gaston,

'Do you think, my dear fellow, you could possibly find us a decent cognac? Something with a touch of anno Domini to it, eh?' The old boy unscrewed the top of his cane, which turned out to be a sort of chunky silver goblet, and handed it over to Gaston, who ducked down among the bottles on the bottom shelf of the trolley and came up with an unopened bottle of Napoleon XO.

'You will all join me?' Bélizon said in a manner that was more of a command than an invitation. After Gaston had set out the brandy balloons and poured us each a decent measure, the old man raised his chalice in salute and said, 'Your very good health.' But he waited watchfully until one of two of us had tasted the stuff before he himself took a tentative sip of his own and then added quietly, 'And mine, too.'

'Perhaps I might do a few introductions,' I suggested, more to break the silence than anything else.

'By all means,' he said, poking his conk appreciatively into the neck of his cup. 'Start with your good self.'

'Jack Devenish is my name, Mr President, and that over there is Ted Arden. We're residents of this humble establishment.'

'You have my deepest sympathy, gentlemen.'

'Yes, well, and perhaps I should first have introduced Madame . . .'

'Madame Diana Lacombe,' he interrupted. 'We are old acquaintances. How are you, Madame Lacombe? Any news of your husband?' At this, Diana went pale as pastry and dug her fingers into the little moppet's arms, hard enough to make her squeal. Bélizon cackled and went on, 'What a charming infant – one can almost fancy a family resemblance there. You must visit my country again soon, Madame. I have a number of policemen who are eager to entertain you. They are rough, coarse fellows, but I am sure they could hold your attention for, say, a week or so – my word, they could.' Diana shuddered and scooped the child up into her arms.

'Please excuse me,' she said, 'but it is long past this young lady's bedtime.' And she swept off back to the annexe.

'Do feel free to rejoin us later,' Bélizon called after her, with a chuckle. Then he turned to Alfie and said, 'And the driver. I must congratulate you, sir, on your survival to such a ripe old age. A remarkable achievement.'

'My name is Petrosian,' Alfie told him.

'Ah, the famous Armenian entrepreneur. Tell me, what *is* the going rate for a John Deere crankshaft in Havana these days?'

It was at this point I noticed that the idiot Horowitz had whipped out a notepad and a biro. Bélizon spotted it at the same time and said, opening his eyes wide,

'Well, now, what have we here? A gentleman of the press, I suspect. Which particular organ do you grace with your talents?'

'I'm kind of what you might call a freelance, Mr President. My name is Horowitz, Jay Horowitz. I was hoping to be able to ask you maybe a coupla questions.'

'And you're an American, by the sound of it.'

'Yes, indeed, sir.'

'Home of the brave, land of the free. Or is it the other way round? I can never remember. So what is it you're burning to ask me?'

'Well, er, that is, when do you foresee a return to democracy in your country?'

'Never, by the grace of God. Democracy is a plague and a curse.'

'Pardon me?' Horowitz could hardly believe his ears.

'Democracy is the product of envy, a most unsavoury emotion to my way of thinking. Democracy leads inevitably to the suppression of the minority. You have only to look at the situation of blacks in your own country. Democracy is mob rule. In the words of that great Irishman, George Bernard Shaw, "Democracy substitutes election by the incompetent many for appointment by the corrupt few." Speaking as one of the corrupt few, I wish to have no truck with it.'

'But that's ridiculous.'

'You only think so because you are an American, and a white American at that. You have been brought up to believe that democracy is an ideal, a holy state of nature. All men are created equal and should have an equal voice. It is a reflex response with you, unquestioned.'

Horowitz was gaping like a landed carp. 'You don't believe in equality?'

'Nobody believes in equality. It is a patently absurd concept to say that all men are equal. Show me just *two* men who are equal. Two men of equal height, weight, eyesight, intelligence, attractiveness to the opposite sex, athletic ability, musical skills. Show me two horses that are equal – two pineapples that are equal. Show me two grains of sand that are equal.'

116

'But damn it,' Ted chipped in, 'all men have equal rights as human beings, surely?'

'Human rights?' Bélizon leaned back in his chair and took another sip of cognac. 'Was there ever a more fatuous collection of words in the history of mankind?' The old boy laughed quite a lot at that, which really pissed Horowitz off.

'We sure as hell know it's a pretty meaningless phrase in your country,' the American told him.

'Well, well, this is clearly going to be an objective piece of journalism. Perhaps we should change the subject. Politics is always something of a minefield.'

'You got plenty of those, too, from what I hear,' murmured Horowitz. The old man ignored this and straightened his collar.

'Now look at this shirt, will you? Isn't it a beauty? D'you know how you can tell a really top-notch Hawaiian shirt? Look at the pocket. See, here, see how the pattern matches? That means it's a first-rate example. Means it hasn't been knocked up on the cheap. You need more fabric, you see, to make a matching pocket.'

'How can you sit there talking about shirts,' protested Horowitz, 'when the wholesale torture and murder of your own people is going on day after day in your name and on your orders?'

Well, that put a bit of a damper on the conversation, as you can well imagine. Horowitz put his head in his hands and moaned quietly for a bit and I noticed that Bélizon was watching this big shiny beetle crawling along the lip of the veranda steps. He sat perfectly still as it made its way towards him and then with a speed I'd have thought well beyond the old boy, he stomped on it with the heel of his boot. When he lifted his foot again, there was this splatter of red and brown on the decking and Ted, God bless him, said quietly,

'Why on earth did you do that? It was harmless.'

'It was a beetle, Mr . . . Arden, is it? Only a beetle. There are more species of beetle on earth than any other creature. Did you know that? One beetle more or less is hardly a tragedy.'

'But it was *alive*,' Ted insisted and got to his feet. 'Please excuse me, I suddenly feel very tired. I must turn in.' He stumbled off towards the door.

'The sanctity of life,' Bélizon called after him, 'is that what concerns you? Let me show you something.' He reached up to his shirt pocket and pulled out that big black fountain pen. Ted paused wearily on the threshold and slowly turned back to look. 'You see this?' the old rascal went on, his little yellow eyes glittering in the lamplight. 'This is the world's finest fountain pen – it costs around four hundred dollars in Miami – it represents a tiny pinnacle of human ingenuity, a masterpiece of engineering. Now watch.' And he placed it very carefully on the floor next to the wreckage of the beetle and then brought his foot down on it.

There was a loud crack and black ink squirted out all round the sole of his boot – I imagine the stain must still be on the plank to this day. He looked around at our astonished faces and called across to Ted, 'So which is the greater loss? The beetle or the pen?' To tell you the truth, I could sort of see what he was getting at, which probably says something about our materialistic society. Or about my own impoverished condition and how I'd forked out nearly four-hundred dollars for Hortense's party frock not twelve hours previously. But Ted just looked him straight in the eye and said very quietly, before taking his leave,

'But how will you replace the beetle?'

CHAPTER FIFTEEN

That night, Arden has a dream. He is walking along an endless, moonlit gallery with closed doors on one side and open French windows on the other. Pale curtains billow round his head and somewhere, far away, he can hear muffled laughter. Two, maybe three voices. He knows the voices are mocking him, but he does not feel threatened. As he passes each door he is aware that it opens behind him, but when he turns to look back he is too slow and the door is already closing again. Coming towards him is a hooded figure, pushing a heavy serving trolley topped with an enormous silver dome. He knows he must reach the trolley but he finds it increasingly difficult to walk, his feet are held back by something. He looks down and finds that he is in his pyjamas and wading knee-deep through a glittering, wriggling carpet of live, stranded fish. The bottoms of his striped trousers are wet and he thinks to himself that in the morning when he wakes they will smell of fish. He staggers to the trolley and lifts the silver dome. Beneath it, in a foetal curl, the naked brown body of Polly lies in a pool of glutinous golden fluid. He does not know if she is sleeping or if she is dead.

He wakes into the blackness of his room and lies motionless, patiently restoring the weft of reality. He can hear voices, laughter. He opens his window and listens behind the closed shutters. Somewhere below on the veranda, he can hear the murmur of conversation. He cannot make out words, but he can smell cigar smoke and he recognizes one of the voices as Bélizon's. He checks his watch in the sliver of moonlight that falls through the crack between the shutters and sees that it is not yet one o'clock. The conversation grows louder and as he eases open the shutters he hears Bélizon say,

'Did you say your name was Horowitz?'

'Yes, sir.'

'You are a Jew, I take it?'

'My family is Jewish, yes. I am not a practising Jew. I am not an orthodox Jew.'

'I don't like Jews.'

'You don't like Jews?'

In the silence that follows, Arden hears only the creak of a chair.

'That is correct,' Bélizon replies eventually. 'I don't like Jews.'

'You admit to being anti-Semitic?'

'Does that surprise you? I suppose it is something of a rarity in this day and age to express such a view. In the thirties it was a most fashionable stance among the British upper classes.'

'And what exactly is it you don't like about us?' Horowitz persists. Bélizon sighs.

'Where to begin? Where to begin? I dislike your unjustifiable smugness, your secretiveness, your ruthless self-serving exclusion of anyone outside your tribe. Back in the thirties if I had stood up and said I don't want my daughter to marry a repulsive fat Jew-boy like you, nobody would have batted an eyelid. Today, because of all that Nazi nonsense I would be condemned as a racist and an anti-Semite. Yet any Jewish father who says, "I don't want my daughter marrying a goy," is supposed to be practising freedom of religion.'

'Which you're also against, I guess?'

'Most certainly I am. I do not encourage freedom of religion. I do not allow superstition to interfere with the smooth running of the state.'

'By "Nazi nonsense" I assume you were referring to the holocaust?' Horowitz's voice sounds pinched and strained.

'The holocaust, yes, that is what it's called these days, isn't it? You know something funny? It's now against the law in Germany to publish a book that says that the holocaust never happened. Imagine that. Against the law. What would they do, do you think, with such a book?' Arden hears gentle wheezy laughter, then, 'Do you think they would have to *burn* it? Now that would be an irony for you.'

'I'm sorry, but I don't find anything remotely amusing in what you say.' There is a long pause, before Bélizon continues,

'But all this is entirely academic. We have no Jewish problem in New Carabali.'

'How come?'

'We have no Jews.'

'None at all? What happened to them?'

'They emigrated years ago.'

'Voluntarily?'

'The majority went of their own accord, yes. Following one or two isolated instances of coercion. Jewish bodies began showing up in remote mountain areas, with all the bones in their bodies smashed. It was a real mystery. What transpired in the end was that some of my troops had become a touch over-zealous and had begun throwing Jews out of helicopters over the central massif. They called it "flying lessons".' He chortles to himself at the memory of it. 'They are such scamps, those boys, such *scallywags*. There was quite a stink about it, internationally, I can tell you. People even talked about a second holocaust. Quite flattering, really.'

Arden silently closes his shutters and the voices become muted and indistinct once more. When he wakes in the morning he cannot easily determine what was dream and what was real, but there is the taste of bile in his mouth and his mind is filled with bleak thoughts.

CHAPTER SIXTEEN

I couldn't be doing with all that political bollocks from the old man. I mean, some of the things he was saying that night out on the veranda made your blood run cold. Horowitz seemed prepared to hang on till dawn, but I made my excuses shortly after that business with the fountain pen and left the pair of them to it. I found Gaston in the kitchen, sitting across the table from Winston. There was a half-empty bottle of hooch between them and they were both as tight as ticks.

'Tell me something,' I asked the bodyguard. 'If Bélizon's so sodding down on whitey, how come he's got a big ugly Boer like Van der Pump looking after him?' Winston sort of giggled and said,

'Best man for the job, is all. Best man for the job. Alphonse pays him top dollar. Us niggers just get to carry out the trash.'

'And taste the rum?'

'I got no complaints, man,' he said and went off into another fit of the giggles. I poured myself a snort and sat down.

'Is he really worried about being poisoned?' I asked.

'Sure certain thing. Wouldn't be the first time, neither. You ever hear tell of the poison arrow frog?'

'Can't say I've ever come across one,' I told him.

'Best for you, you don't. Most poisonous creatures known to man. Little black and yellow buggers, just 'bout big as your thumb. Each frog got maybe two hundred micrograms of poison on its body. You get just a couple of them micrograms down you, you a dead man. Just one lick of the skin and it's lights out. The Indians use the stuff on their arrows – that how come it gets the name.'

'Evil fucker, sounds like,' Gaston slurred, which set Winston off again. When he stopped laughing he said in a deadly serious tone,

'No, but one time, I'm telling you, someone tried to use it to kill the boss man. Formal dinner, it was, in the presidential palace. Clever part was, they didn't touch the food. They just smeared the stuff on his fork. Would have worked, too, only he got spooked 'cos his seat was too near the window – thought someone might think to take a pot shot at him. So he swapping places with the minister of sport.' Winston thought this was hilarious. Splitting his sides, he was. 'The man dropping down stone dead after the first forkful. From that day to this, the old bastard always carry his cutlery around with him. Always new, out of canteens he keep in his private safe. Use only once and chuck in the bin. Same with drinking glasses. Got that big old silver goblet on his walking cane. Never drink from nothin' else.'

'Shit,' Gaston gasped, 'that is one very careful *mec*, I am thinking.'

'They find out who did it?' I asked.

'No way. But he shoot a few people anyway, just for appearances. Show he not going soft or nothing.'

I staggered up to bed shortly after this illuminating little exchange and managed to get one shoe off before passing out. When I woke up next morning it was gone eleven o'clock and the inside of my mouth seemed to be lined with rabbit fur and my teeth felt loose and crumbly. There was a hell of a racket coming from somewhere outside, motorbikes roaring, car doors slamming and the hollow, echoey voices of walkie-talkies barking back and forth to one another. Turned out the French delegation had arrived with full military escort, not wishing to be upstaged by the visiting team, I suppose. Gaston had told me that both sides were going to be sequestered away all day in the old ballroom at the north end of the villa, presumably discussing vital affairs of state and what-have-you. Or maybe they were just going to watch blue movies and drink beer.

129

In any event, your humble storyteller had promised Alfie the night before that I'd take myself down to the port for one of his breakfast restoratives. I treated myself to a clean shirt and a change of socks, although I'm bound to admit that the old gabardine suit would not have passed muster in the Royal Enclosure at Ascot. I sponged it down a bit and shook it out over the balcony to freshen it up before I put it on, but I was still picking up a telltale whiff of cheap cigars and stale anisette. Well, couldn't be helped. In any event, doesn't do for a man to take too much care over his appearance, I always think. Suggests a frivolous disposition and an idle mind. Or, in Ted's case, something worse.

When I hit the *Macaque Agile*, the magic potion was ready and waiting for me on the corner of the bar. The Bloody Mary à la Petrosian. Best pick-me-up known to civilized man. Alfie once divulged the secret recipe, which I now pass on to you free of charge on the sole condition that you buy me one if you're ever passing through. Here goes. Tall narrow glass, two big ice cubes. Sprinkle the ice cubes *liberally* with coarsely ground cayenne pepper – do not use Tabasco: too vinegary. Juice of half a fresh lime, five dashes of Lea & Perrin's Worcestershire Sauce, and no more than a teaspoonful of dry sherry – manzanilla for preference, on account of the slight saltiness – plus half a teaspoonful of celery salt. Fill the glass one third full with vodka – any vodka will do, the cheaper the better – you're not going to be tasting it. Stirring vigorously, pour in the tomato juice from a fair height to blend with all the other stuff. The tomato juice should be the thickest you can find and it should be chilled to within an inch of its life. Fish out the ice cubes and discard. Consume.

It's like drinking a frozen volcano. It can restore the departed to life. It is the elixir of Lazarus. It is the resurrection before death. It's a flaming miracle. I drank two and the world was filled with joy once more and an inexplicable optimism pervaded all my thoughts. Alfie stood back and watched the performance critically, like a painter admiring his brushwork, and he beamed when I slapped the second empty glass down on the zinc.

'By God, but that hit the spot,' I told him. He nodded and lit up one of his noxious gaspers. No idea where he imports them from but they smell like someone set fire to a badger.

'I tell you one funny thing,' he said, leaning forward over the counter in a conspiratorial sort of a way. 'When I get back here last night, there's this guy . . .'

'What guy?'

'Big guy, tall, taller than you, Hispanic type. Wearing this chunky gold ring with a cabochon emerald in it, big as an olive. Made me think he was maybe Colombian. Had a beard, too, big black beard. And he was drunk, very drunk. He was sitting down the end there, drinking tequila on the rocks and hanging on to the bar like he was on board ship in heavy seas. And he had a whole heap of American money, roll of twenty-dollar bills as thick as your arm. You know what he told me?'

'What did he tell you?'

'He told me he was a killer. Professional killer. Like it might be a hit man, you could say. Came right out with it. Told me just like that.'

'Which almost certainly means it wasn't true.'

'You didn't see him. Anyway, he says to me, "Are you not the man who is driving President Bélizon up into the hills?" So I tell him, yes this is me. And you know what he says then, very quiet? He says, "You won't be driving him back down again." I tell you, Jack, it put the willies right up me, way he said it, and all.'

'Sounds like a load of old cobblers to me. What sort of a contract killer goes around getting drunk and telling everybody what he's up to? I reckon he was pulling your plonker.'

'I don't think so, I don't think so. He was very tough, very scary. Maybe it's some drug thing, you know. Something like that.'

When I got back to the Auberge, I stepped out onto my

balcony for a breath of fresh air before lunch and who should I see but Van der Pump standing further along on the President's own balcony, peering up into the hills through these enormous field glasses. I cleared my throat and he swivelled round to fix me with his little rosy peepers.

'Sorry, old man,' I said, 'didn't mean to startle you.'

'What's *your* problem?' he asked.

'No problem at all, that I'm aware of. You might have one, though,' I told him, emboldened by the Petrosian life-savers.

'Meaning?'

'There's some chap down in the port telling all and sundry he's got a contract to kill your guv'nor. South American feller, big bloke with a beard.'

'When was this?' he asked, and looked at his watch.

'Late last night. He was in Alfie Petrosian's bar, throwing his money around and talking tough.'

'I am obliged to you for this piece of intelligence, Mr Devenish,' he said eventually. 'I believe I know the identity of the individual you describe. We shall take the appropriate measures, rest assured.' And with that, he turned on his heel and went back inside. Cool customer. Although in the light of what happened later, perhaps a bit too cool for his own good.

CHAPTER SEVENTEEN

The banquet is to begin at seven-thirty with drinks on the veranda. All afternoon, Magali toils away alongside her *brigade de cuisine* in the sweltering heat of the kitchen. As usual she listens to her adored Brassens at full volume. She drifts in and out of a nostalgic reverie as the familiar words wash over her, the story of *Jeanne*, a saint-like, white-haired innkeeper whose '*auberge est ouverte aux gens sans feu ni lieu*'. This is how Magali likes to imagine herself in old age, as a frail, spiritual presence, *la mère universelle*, offering hospitality and refuge to the humblest of God's creatures. She sings along at the top of her lungs, '*Chez Jeanne, la Jeanne / On est n'importe qui, on vient n'importe quand / Et, comme par miracle, par enchantement / On fait parti' de la famille*,' and as she sings, she weeps at the memory of her own poor family in Marseille, kilometres away and years ago. The music ends and she wipes away her tears, looking sharply about her to make sure that nobody has been watching her and that every nose is still firmly applied to the grindstone. Over in one corner,

Winston sprawls in a chair, having succumbed once more to a surfeit of rum. She sees the almost-empty bottle where it has rolled beneath his chair, listens to the mucous rumbling of his snores and her heart is filled with fury.

'How dare these people invade *my* world like this?' she mutters to herself. 'What gives them the right to question *my* methods, to test *my* dishes for poison? How dare this great *gorille* waddle round *my* kitchen, poking his nose – and his greasy fat fingers – into *my* business and drinking *my* fine vintage rum? Poison is it, they are worried about? *Eh bien*, I'll show them poison.'

She has devised a plan, a way to bring chaos and confusion to the party. Something to teach them all a lesson. She has commanded Gaston to serve a special cocktail at the start of the evening. It is to be a traditional old English gin sling, in honour of the Auberge's loyal residents. But as a token of unity with the French nation, the gin and cherry brandy will be mixed not with lemonade or soda, but with vintage Bollinger. Served in heavy crystal rummers, each innocuous-tasting draught will deliver the alcoholic kick of a half-bottle of champagne with a large gin in it.

Then, as an *amuse-gueule* she will serve slivers of home-smoked red snapper with horseradish sauce and large glasses of frozen aquavit *à la Norvégienne*. 'Their brains will be

136

spinning in their skulls,' she thinks to herself with a sly smile. After which will come the coup de grâce. A chilled beetroot soup, a variant on the Russian *svekolnik* with cucumber and sour cream, but instead of adding a traditional glass of the mildly intoxicating kvass, she will introduce a double shot of Polish spirit to each bowl. 'They will be passing out on the parquet before the fish course,' she tells herself gleefully.

At around five, Gaston emerges from the cellar where he has been selecting wines to accompany the main courses, and he is a far from happy man.

'*Les salauds!*' he exclaims, slapping the flat of his hand against the cellar doorframe. 'A whole case they have taken!'

'Who has taken what, you old fleabag?' Magali asks.

'Rum,' he hisses back at her. 'Those *emmerdeurs* of body-guards have stolen a whole case of rum.' He takes up a wide-legged stance in front of Winston, leans forward and bellows into his sleeping face. 'Where is my rum, *you sack of shit*?'

Winston's lids flutter open, but the unfocused eyeballs within swivel helplessly in their sockets, straining to impart some shred of usable information to his befuddled brain.

'Rum?' he eventually manages to croak. He gropes fruit-lessly under his chair for the bottle.

'Rum? You give it me last night. We sit there at the table, get drunk together with good old Jack Devenish.'

Magali snorts,

'Much more like the true story, way I see it.'

'I am not talking about a couple of glasses,' screams Gaston, 'I'm talking about a whole fucking case! Twelve fucking bottles.'

'I swear to God,' protests Winston, 'I never touch nothing. Only what you give me, man.' Gaston, breathing hard, studies the perspiring bodyguard closely, and tells him,

'From this moment on, I am watching you and your friends. First one of you I catch in that cellar gets buried down there. That understood?'

Winston peers blearily up at him and says,

'Gotta take a leak.' The bemused bodyguard totters out through the back door, massaging the top of his skull with his chubby fingertips and after he has gone Gaston crosses to the dresser drawer and unwraps the Desert Eagle. He tucks it into the waistband at the back of his trousers beneath his shirt and slams the chair down in front of the cellar door.

'There,' he tells Magali, 'is where I am spending the night. Nobody ain't getting no more free rum.'

She smirks to herself over the chopping board. There are

times when Gaston seems to her pretty good value, for all his damn idleness.

Arden spends the afternoon up at the rock pool with Diana and Polly. As ever the child has stripped off and plunges repeatedly into the green depths, shrieking and whooping with unrestrained delight. Arden sits with his back to the water so as not to see the glistening brown body that continues to haunt and disturb him.

'Isn't it strange,' Diana asks, 'how we none of us really belong here, on this island?'

'I feel that I belong here as much as anywhere,' he replies.

'But don't you have the sense that we're all somehow stranded here, like the survivors of a shipwreck? Even though we've each of us chosen to be here for our own reasons, none of us really and truly *belongs*. The French don't belong here. Poor Magali is desperately homesick for Marseille. You and Jack are very far from your green and pleasant homeland. Only dear little Polly there has a right to call this place her home.'

'But you were born out here, you said.'

'Yes,' she smiles gently, 'but it was a different time. And different times make different places.'

'In any case, I'm not sure I feel myself to be particularly English. I don't really know what being English means.'

'Jack seems to believe that England is some sort of mental attitude, a state of mind. Something you carry about with you wherever you go in the world. Something to do with civilized values.'

'Perhaps he's right. I've always thought that the one thing you could say about an Englishman is that he would always know the right thing to do in a given situation. The decent thing.'

'Even if he didn't always do it? Do you think you'll ever go back?'

'I don't think that I could now. Not after everything that's happened.'

'You mean your friend – what was her name – Rebecca? Do you feel that you have to stay here for her sake, to be close to the life you had together?' She looks steadily into his eyes. 'Do you think she might still be alive?'

'I don't suppose I do, really. I overheard Bélizon talking last night, after I'd gone up to my room.' Out of the corner of his eye he catches sight of Polly's brown body in midair and remembers his dream. 'The man is a festering anti-Semite,' he goes on. 'You hear such stories about what's been happening to the Jews in New Carabali. Terrible, terrible stories.'

'I'm afraid those stories are mostly true.'

'Rebecca was Jewish, of course.'

'Yes.' She holds out her hand to him and he squeezes it between both of his. 'I am so very sorry.'

'What happened to your husband? Why did Bélizon mention him last night?'

'Similar story to yours, I suppose. Except that Didier really was involved in politics, and so we both knew what might happen to him. He was out here with the Red Cross on some sort of fact-finding mission, but once you see what's going on, it's impossible to remain neutral. Impossible not to get drawn in. He was simply caught in the wrong place at the wrong time. And, more importantly, with the wrong people.'

'Do you know what happened to him?'

'No. Like you, I can only wonder. And imagine.'

CHAPTER EIGHTEEN

Hortense showed up in the front entrance hall just after seven, looking like a pretty sizeable percentage of a million dollars. The frock was a skin-tight electric blue satin sheath that stretched over her rear end like the paint job on a Maserati. She'd festooned herself about with glittery sparklers, could even have been real diamonds, I suppose – generous client or two – and she wore these strappy gilt leather sandals with glass heels about six inches high. Her eyelids and fingernails looked like they'd been gold-plated. She gave me a big sticky kiss and looked around the hall.

'Takes me back some, seein' all this, Jack. Place gone down the hill a bit since my time.'

'You know the old Auberge, then?' I asked her.

'Worked here for a bit. One of my times trying to go straight, like you might say. Got a job in the linen room, sorting through the dirty bedsheets. Di'n last long, though. Money was shit, work was hard. So I went back to me old job of making the sheets dirty in the first place.'

I led her through to the veranda, where Gaston had draped a couple of trestle tables in white damask cloths and set out rows of heavy glasses and three huge punchbowls full of some frothy-looking brew. There were already a few of the French delegation standing awkwardly about in their monkey suits with drinks in their hands, pretending to have a good time. Hortense turned her back on them and wiggled her electric blue arse and you could hear the ice cubes rattling in their glasses.

Gaston handed us a drink each and said under his breath,

'Take it easy, *les copains*. This is high-octane rocket fuel, I deceive you not at all.' Tasted like fruit cup to me, but I always deferred to Gaston on the subject of strong drink. Hard-headedest man I ever met. Could drink any three other men under the table, even if they were working in shifts. I passed on his warning to Hortense and she sniffed her glass.

'Pussy piss,' she said with a shrug, and knocked it back in one. Gaston rolled his eyes to the heavens and filled her up again.

'*Mademoiselle*,' he said with a little bow, '*mes compliments*.'

Ted showed up five minutes later with Diana clinging to his elbow, as usual. I'm bound to say, she looked absolutely stunning. Plain black velvet cocktail dress and a string of baroque pearls. Then, bugger me if she and Hortense didn't start hugging and kissing like a couple of long-lost sisters and gabbing away nineteen to the dozen in some jungle gibberish, while Ted and I just stood there having about as much fun as a pair of one-legged men at an arse-kicking party. So much for my cunning ruse to ferment a hotbed of seething jealousy.

'You two know each other, then?' I asked Hortense casually, when they finally broke from the clinch.

'You best believe it, Jacky boy,' she said. 'Me and Lady Diana here go way, way back. In my book, she the next best thing to that Mother Teresa.'

'Hardly,' Diana said, flushing, 'but I am truly grateful for your enormous generosity over the years. Hortense,' she explained to the rest of us, 'has sponsored several of my little charges. She's even paying to put one through medical school in Chicago.'

'Heavens above,' I protested in mock horror, 'don't tell me she has the proverbial heart of gold.'

'Watch your mouth, Jack Devenish. I maybe got teeth of gold, and you'd do well to remember that.' She turned back to Diana and asked, 'So how are all them other little Polly girls of yours makin' out? You got a new one, from what I been hearin'.'

'I most certainly have, Hortense,' Diana told her with a trilling little laugh, 'and believe me, this one is a real handful. She can't keep her hands off poor Mr Arden here.' Hortense gave Ted a bit of an old-fashioned look, but of course, I didn't twig anything. Not then.

Guitry came rolling up at that moment, bowed formally to Diana and kissed her hand like a joke Frenchman in a Whitehall farce.

'Madame Lacombe,' he said in that oily way he had, 'I am the most fortunate of men to have such a charming dinner companion.' He reached into his inside jacket pocket with his spare hand, 'I believe these documents will be of some use to your charming young protégée. You should find everything in order.' And he passed over a stiffish brown envelope. Diana slipped it into her handbag without opening it and gave him a cool smile.

'This is most welcome news, Monsieur Guitry, and a great relief. We were just talking about Polly, weren't we? I'm sorry, do you know everybody? Hortense, may I . . .' Hortense flashed her pearly-white choppers and took Guitry's hand.

'I heard tell of Monsieur Guitry, of course,' she said in a throaty warble, 'but sadly I ain't never had the pleasure. You had the pleasure lately, Monsieur Guitry?' The poor fellow looked like he was struggling to swallow a live toad. Gaston handed round more drinks and I tipped Ted the wink.

'Go easy on this stuff,' I warned him, 'Gaston says it's pure nitroglycerine.' But Ted seemed miles away. He just nodded and took a long deep swig.

'How did the negotiations go today?' Diana asked Guitry, who was still trying to regain his bureaucratic sang-froid.

'*Hélas*, not entirely according to plan, Madame Lacombe. I fear that President Bélizon's expectations were a little more ambitious than we had anticipated.'

'Wanted you to hand over the family silver, eh?' I asked him, sort of joshing. But he took it all very seriously.

'He does not seem to realize that if the French government and the World Bank are to provide more funds for New Carabali, we must have some guarantees that the money will be used for humanitarian purposes and not spirited away into some *Stiftung* in Liechtenstein.'

'Or frittered away on a new presidential yacht,' I chipped in.

'Precisely,' Guitry agreed, pulling a big silk hanky out of his sleeve and dabbing away at his neck. 'I only hope he does not decide to make a speech tonight. Some of his speeches have been known to last for six or seven hours. He is as bad as Castro.'

'Funny thing about the yacht,' I told him. 'I was down in the port this morning and there was no sign of the bloody thing. There it was yesterday, out in the middle of the bay, and this morning it's vanished.'

'Really?' Guitry asked. 'How very curious.'

'Don't think somebody's nicked it, do you?' I said as a joke. But Guitry still didn't crack a smile. Instead he looked thoughtfully down into his glass and said,

'Perhaps I had better contact the coastguard.'

The great man himself showed up right then, all dolled up in his best dress uniform, like Gilbert and Sullivan in jackboots. Only touch of incongruity was a knife, fork and spoon sticking out of his top pocket. He was flanked by Van der Pump on one side and by one of his personal minders on the other. A number of swarthy individuals straggled along in his wake, presumably a bunch of his most trusted political advisers. Not that I'd have trusted any man jack of them with so much as the keys to the khazi.

The other guests parted like the Red Sea to let them pass through and Bélizon settled himself down in a big wicker arm-chair, unscrewing the silver chalice from his cane and passing it to Gaston, who filled it up from one of the punchbowls picked out by the minder. The old bastard took a sip and nodded grudgingly as if to say that it just about met with his presidential approval and then his eye lighted on Hortense's cerulean rump, and he said,

'My word, who have we here?' Hortense handed me her glass, sashayed across to his chair with her hands on her hips, thrust what you might call her gynaecological region under his nose and drawled,

'Why, Massa President. Ain't you never done seen no nigger who' befo'? Way I hear it, the old presidential palace stuffed with them. Way I hear it, you got hot and cold running pussy in every room.'

It went awfully quiet at this point in the proceedings and we all waited while she and the old man looked each other squarely in the eye, then with a great whoop, he burst out laughing and started banging his stick on the deck.

'I only wish, young lady. I only wish it were true. Maybe once upon a time, but those days are long gone. My God, though, but you'd have had pride of place, I can tell you that.' Everyone started talking and smiling again and Hortense made herself comfortable on the arm of the old man's chair. I took her glass over to her and Bélizon said,

'Don't tell me you're with *him*.'

'Sure 'nuff am,' she said, taking my hand. 'He my fine sugar daddy, take good care of me.'

'Well, good for you, sir,' he said.

'I gather that things didn't entirely go your way at today's meeting,' I said, struggling to keep a civil tone in my voice.

'On the contrary, Mr Devenish,' he confided with a creepy little smile, 'I obtained rather more than I had expected. Not, needless to say, as much as I asked for, but therein lies the art of negotiation. Demand three times what you need and settle for half of what you demand.'

'With no strings attached?' Diana asked.

149

'Oh, there are always one or two tiresome conditions, but that is all part of the sport. The money will have to be filtered through the usual charitable organizations, I imagine, but it will end up in the right pockets eventually.'

As he was saying this, my eye was caught by the grotesque spectacle of Horowitz, jumping up and down and waving beyond the far end of the veranda rails, evidently trying to attract my attention. I excused myself and toddled off to find out what he was getting so het up about.

'What's the game?' I said, looking pointedly down at his greasy Bermudas. 'This is a private party, you know. Black tie and all that.'

'Somebody's broken into my room, gone through all my things.' He was sweating. He was always sweating.

'Anything missing?' I asked.

'My notebook.'

'Is that all? What about your gold card?'

He shook his head. 'No, that's still there. Only the notebook is missing.'

'Well, there's a stroke of luck, then.'

'But don't you see what this means? This has got to be Bélizon and his scuzzy crew. It's censorship, that's what it is. They don't want the world to learn the truth.'

I caught Van der Pump watching the pair of us from behind

Bélizon's chair. He had this vulpine grin on his face, like a school prefect who'd just caught you having a crafty Woodbine behind the bicycle sheds.

'Truth, what truth?' I asked Horowitz. 'You mean the truth the man's a fascist psychopath? Can't see the *New York Times* holding the front page for that particular scoop, old son.'

'You didn't hear the stuff he was saying after you left last night . . .'

'Pretty strong meat, I daresay, but still and all . . .'

'What do you think I should do about it? I mean, do you think I should report it to someone – the French police maybe?'

'Can't imagine it would do much good, but I'll have a word with Guitry if you like. Best I can promise.'

This seemed to calm the poor chap down and he looked like he was about to push off, but as I turned back to rejoin the party, Bélizon called out from the other end of the veranda,

'Is that the little fat Jew-boy? I do hope he's not joining us for dinner. The sight of his greasy little Yiddish face would quite put a chap off his victuals.'

Horowitz, furious, turned as pale as dripping and lurched towards the presidential group.

'I wouldn't sit down at the same table as you, if I was starving to death,' he shrieked.

'I am much relieved to hear it,' the old man cackled. Horowitz's attempt to mount the veranda steps was stopped short by Winston's fat black paw on his chest.

'Don't worry,' Horowitz jeered over the bodyguard's shoulder. 'I'm no threat. I wouldn't dirty my hands on an anti-Semitic little monkey like you.'

'"Monkey" is it now?' Bélizon asked mildly. 'Such racist abuse. I do believe Mr Horowitz is not quite himself this evening. A touch of the sun, perhaps. These fair-skinned types are particularly susceptible, I'm told.'

'Well, *you* were certainly yourself last night,' the young idiot bawled at him. 'You were very much your goddamn self. Why don't you tell everybody what you told me? Why don't you tell them what a big joke the holocaust was? And while you're on the subject, why don't you tell everybody what happened to all the Jews in *your* country?'

There was, as you might expect, a bit of an awkward silence at this juncture. Bélizon stared down at his boots, like he was embarrassed – not for himself, I got the impression, but for the lardy lad. Winston and Van der Pump frogmarched the poor clodpole off the premises, and that was the last any of us saw of him that night. Or, matter of fact, ever again.

CHAPTER NINETEEN

Alphonse Bélizon finishes his *svekolnik*, leans back into his seat at the head of the long, glittering table and considers his dining companions with a mixture of mistrust and distaste. Beside him, at his insistence, sits Hortense and he supposes that she is harmless enough. And so is the stupid, ugly Englishman on the other side of her. But Guitry is up to something, he is sure of it – he and the Lacombe woman, heads together, hugger-mugger. The day has been long and trying, the residual pain from his old kidney problem thrusting itself forward with pitiless frequency. The negotiations themselves had been suspiciously easy, the French conceding too much, too readily, as though they were expecting him to die before the ink was dry on the paper. Guitry had made a half-hearted attempt at playing hard to get, but you could tell his heart wasn't in it. And they had agreed to the most important condition of all: a military aircraft to fly him to France for treatment with ironclad guarantees of safe conduct. Nothing else matters. The money is beside the point, one could always get money from somewhere.

He looks down to the far end of the table, where Arden, uncomfortably wedged between two members of the French negotiating team, is attempting to engage them in polite conversation. A strange man, Bélizon concludes. Weak and vain, but not without intelligence. What was it he had said the night before? 'How will you replace the beetle?' He observes that Arden is drenched in perspiration, his collar soggy with it and his moustache slick. The man is everything he despises about the British. That absurd combination of arrogance and sentimentality. As he watches, Arden's sleeve upends his wineglass, sending its crimson contents spreading over the tablecloth like a haemorrhage. Seeing the poor man dabbing ineffectually about with his napkin, it occurs to Bélizon that this sad little Englishman is quite drunk.

In this observation, he is correct. Brought to a state of near mental paralysis by the prospect of the evening ahead, Arden has been in his room, fortifying himself with whisky since his return from the rock pool that afternoon. Two tumblersful of Gaston's potent cocktail, followed by the aquavit – rashly knocked back in one – have blunted his inhibitions, buffered his shyness. He catches Bélizon's eye and asks, more loudly than he intends,

'I gather you approve of the holocaust?' After a pause, Bélizon says with a shrug,

'Worse things have happened.'

Devenish can restrain himself no longer.

'What could possibly be worse,' he blusters, 'than the systematic extermination of six million innocent people?'

Bélizon swivels his aqueous, yellow-rimmed eyes to confront the other man and says,

'Mr Devenish, I do not believe I have ever in my entire life encountered an innocent person.' He takes a sip of wine, wipes his reptilian lips fastidiously with his napkin and continues, 'In the years of terror following the Russian revolution Stalin is thought to have killed more than forty-five million of his own people, mostly through starvation. That makes him seven times more wicked than Hitler, one could argue. Under Mao Tse-tung the communist regime in China was responsible for the deaths of more than sixty million people. Ten times the crime, you might say.'

'But,' Arden insists, 'there has to be a difference. None of that's comparable to what happened to the Jews in Germany.'

'Or perhaps you would care for an example from nearer home,' Bélizon continues, ignoring the interruption. 'Well, when the *white*, European Spanish invaders arrived in South

America there were eighty million native inhabitants. Within six generations, there were only ten million left alive. But, you know, the funny thing is, you never hear the Jews complaining about that, do you? Maybe because not too many of those dead aboriginals were called Isaac or Miriam. Is that the "difference" you referred to?'

'It just *feels* different. It just feels terribly, terribly evil to systematically persecute people simply because of their race.'

'Race, Mr Arden? Hitler's extermination of the Jews had nothing to do with race. The Jews are not a race, they are a tribe. The blacks are a race, the Jews are a sort of exclusive club. Membership is voluntary. Do you know in Spain, during the time of the Inquisition, thousands of Jews converted to Christianity? Saint Teresa of Avila was originally a Jewess. Oh, yes, when the men with the red robes and the crucifixes came knocking on the door, what did our crafty Jew-boy say? "Funny you should mention it, but I'm actually a good Catholic, always have been – Ave Maria and God bless the Pope." You try that in Mississippi when the Klan comes calling. You try telling those good old boys in the pointy white cowls, "Nigger, me? Shucks, no, I'm a white man, born and raised, honky through and through and, by the way, can I have the hand of your daughter in marriage?"

Being a Jew is a matter of preference, Mr Arden. Being a nigger is not.'

'But that doesn't make the persecution of the Jews right,' Devenish chips in.

'It makes it . . . understandable. If you spend two or three thousand years strutting about the planet, telling everybody that you are God's chosen people and the rest of humanity is rubbish, you must expect a little local difficulty from time to time.'

'You call the holocaust *a little local difficulty*?' Arden manages to stammer.

'Particularly,' Bélizon persists, 'compared with the fate of the unremembered millions of nameless blacks who were ripped from their homelands in Africa and either died of plague in the slave ships, drowning in their own bloody excrement, or made it to the New World, to be casually flogged to death by an alien people fortified by a religious assurance of their own racial superiority.'

The plates are cleared away, the next course carried in and laid before the guests; *langouste à la vanille aux asperges sauvages*. Bélizon stares down at his plate and winces as a fresh surge of pain constricts his loins. He leans back in his chair momentarily, his eyes closed, before concluding,

'So do not presume, Mr Arden, to lecture me on the subject

of the holocaust. My ancestors were black slaves on my father's side and forest Indians on my mother's. I have to tell you that, from where I sit, the chosen people and the master race are two sides of a very thin coin.'

CHAPTER TWENTY

G od, it was spooky, sitting there, listening to the old bastard trotting out his poisonous opinions. What made it worse was, if you didn't keep your wits about you, you could almost catch yourself going along with some of his ideas. That was the thing about the man. He could trot out the most appalling bollocks and it came across like sound common sense. But then, that's probably how these dictators come to power in the first place. The gift of the gab, making white look black, as you might say.

'Don't it worry you none,' Hortense suddenly asked him, 'the massive gap between the richest people in your country and all the strugglin' poor?'

'It doesn't worry *me*, my dear,' he said, leaning back in his chair and patting her hand. 'Maybe it worries *them*, although I don't see why it should.'

'No?' Diana challenged him. 'Your agricultural workers earn an average of twelve US dollars a month in your cane fields. You spend more than that on a single cigar.'

'Are they really paid that much? You are better informed than I am, Madame Lacombe. Well, nobody forces them to work. And I fail to see what the price of my cigars has to do with the issue. If they are happy to labour for that wage, then why should they concern themselves with what others earn? It can only make them resentful and unhappy. Remember the parable of the workers in the vineyard; there is much wisdom in the gospels, if you know where to look for it.' He passed his cup to one of the waitresses for a top-up and went on, 'As I say, this concept of equality – all these dangerous notions of democracy – are the product of envy, pure and simple. And envy, my friends, makes people unhappy. Read your excellent Bertrand Russell – biggest single cause of unhappiness in the world, envy – according to him.'

Hortense nudged me in the ribs just after the lobster plates were cleared away and murmured,

'I reckon the old boy got real gyp over here.'

'How d'you mean?'

'He got terrible pain somewhere. You can tell.'

'Couldn't happen to a nicer feller,' I told her, and then I asked Guitry, 'What time are these fireworks, then?' He hauled out a fat gold pocket watch and said,

'Ten-thirty, I believe. In just over one hour's time. We shall be able to see them from the veranda.'

'Not sure I can stay awake,' I said. 'Gaston's cocktails have just about done for me. How many more courses have we got?' At which point, Arden decided to get stuck in again. Dutch courage, I suppose.

'And I imagine, Mr President,' he said, 'there is absolutely no truth in these allegations of atrocities being committed in your own country?' He sounded quite pissed, I thought, a bit on the slurry side, so the word 'atrocities' was quite an adventure for him.

'Atrocities?' said the old boy, going a bit bug-eyed, as if he hadn't heard properly. 'Oh, there are certainly occasional atrocities. They are bound to happen, even in the best-regulated societies.' He leaned forward, and looked round the table with a broad grin on his face. 'I must tell you the latest, by the way. This will amuse you. It seems that some of my soldiers invented a game called "pudding roulette" – have you heard about this? No? Well, apparently they were arresting pregnant Indian women and taking bets amongst themselves on the sex of the unborn children. When the kitty got big enough they'd slit open the woman's belly and take a butcher's at the foetus. Unfortunate choice of words, perhaps.'

By a gruesome coincidence that was when they chose to bring on the next course, one of Magali's specialities. It's a

161

dish called, if I've got it right, '*Poularde de Bresse truffée en vessie Joannes Nandron*' and under normal circumstances, it's a real cracker. Takes the form of whole chickens, stuffed with truffles and minced veal soaked in Madeira. Only thing is, each of the noble birds is then poached in a whole inside-out pig's bladder. They bring them to the table on a big carving trolley and slice open the bladders before your very eyes before cutting up the chicken and sharing it out.

'Oh my dear God!' Ted gasped, when they lifted up the lid and Gaston plunged his carving knife into the first of the pale, wobbly bladders. 'That is utterly appalling . . .' You know, I thought he was going to chuck up, but he looked away and somehow held it together.

'Yes, awful, isn't it?' Bélizon agreed with that irritating little laugh of his. 'But they're such imps, such *rascals*. It couldn't be allowed to go on, of course. I had the whole bunch of them rounded up and shot – no choice, really. I'm afraid the United Nations takes a very dim view of such shenanigans. Crimes against humanity, they call it, or some such gibberish. I mean, how can anyone commit a crime against humanity? Are we not all of us human beings? I certainly am, you all appear to be. So how could any of us commit a crime against humanity? We *are* humanity. I could commit a crime against one of you, you could commit a crime against me – it's all a matter of law. But a crime against humanity? It's a meaningless phrase.

'But you see, they're so sloppy with language, these international lawyers. Before you know where you are, they've turned their gobbledygook into law and then you have sanctions and indictments and extradition treaties and heaven knows what other kinds of foolishness. Human rights? What does that mean? If you grant me the right to graze my sheep on your land, that is something I understand. But who grants human rights? God? Not much evidence of that, I would submit – certainly not the kind of evidence that would stand up in The Hague. No, it's like all of these other wretched so-called "rights". Women's rights, gay rights, animal rights, children's rights. Who has granted these rights? Who is in a position to determine that a person is born with any rights whatsoever?' And with that he raised his cup and announced,

'Here's to the British Empire and all who went down with her.'

'I am not ashamed of my country's history,' I told him, straight out.

'Nor should you be, dear boy. Greatest empire the world has ever seen, one fifth of the world's population at one time was under British rule, did you know that? One person in five. Extraordinary to think of that now. And do you know how it was accomplished? Not through democracy, believe me. Oh dear me, no. It was through strong men, firm leadership.' He sighed. 'All gone now, of course.'

'We are still a force to be reckoned with,' I told him, conscious that I was sounding just a touch bombastic. 'I think the Falklands war proved that.'

'The Falklands? You speak, of course, in jest. One insignificant little island group squabbling over another. You give away the greatest empire the world has ever seen – piss it up against the wall. Africa, India, America, the Far East. You just let it slip through your fingers. And then when Argentina tries to claim a few square miles of worthless, guano-spattered rock in the south Atlantic, you all start jumping up and down and sending in the gunboats. Good grief, man, British Guiana was *twelve times* the size of the Falklands and you just wrapped it up in a ribbon and handed it over to the biggest bunch of crooks this side of Medellin.'

'I think you will find that Guyana is still part of the British Commonwealth,' Diana quietly pointed out to him.

'Which means what, Madame, precisely?'

'I believe that the Commonwealth can exert a civilizing influence on the global community,' Diana said evenly. 'I believe it can uphold moral values.'

'Moral values, you say?' Bélizon smiled to himself. 'Well,

I'm afraid there you have lost me. I am a soldier and a politician. I cannot afford the luxury of moral values. Unlike your own native politicians, of course, with their fine talk of ethical foreign policies. When India and Pakistan announce that they are both testing atomic weapons, what does *Great* Britain do about it? Eh? I mean, here you have two Commonwealth countries threatening each other with hydrogen bombs, and so what does your noble and fearless Foreign Office actually do? It puts on its sternest face, bangs on the table and *condemns* them.

'Imagine that. Two mighty nations – more than a billion people and the British government *condemns* their actions. How they must have been quaking in their boots. Imagine their terror: "Oh my God, we'd better not test any more bombs in case that dreary little island off the northwest coast of Europe decides to *condemn* us again." I must confess I do find it all most amusing although, in a way, it's also terribly sad.

'The problem is, of course,' he rambled on, 'the British no longer have leaders. They have government by opinion poll. No decision is made without first canvassing the views of the great unwashed proletariat, for fear of courting unpopularity. And where do the great unwashed get their views? Why, from the tabloid newspapers. The press barons tell the public what to think and the public tells the government what to do.

'Consider this wretched business of fox-hunting. Just think of the parliamentary time and taxpayers' money the British government has expended trying to decide whether or not a handful of people can dress up in red coats to hunt foxes from horseback. It's absurd, ludicrous. It's like something out of *Gulliver's Travels*. And all because the uneducated cretins who read the tabloid newspapers don't like to think of an upper-class minority enjoying itself. Envy, pure envy. But that is the inevitable way of things in a democracy. The minority always suffers.'

'Do you not have opinion polls in your country, Mr President?' Diana piped up in the awkward hush that followed.

'What would be the point? What possible interest could I have in the views of the uninformed masses? It is a delusion to believe that wisdom resides in the majority view. A million morons are no more intelligent than a single moron. My people know they can rely on me to make decisions on their behalf, just as children rely on their parents to decide what is best for them.'

And with that, the old bastard slumped back in his seat, folded his hands across his chest and closed his eyes for all the world like he was about to take a nap. The conversation slowly picked up round the table, after a fashion, but nobody really seemed to know what to talk about. Fact of the matter is,

everyone was half cut and it was getting pretty hard to follow
what was being said, particularly by the French mob with their
usual arrogant reluctance to speak the Queen's English.

CHAPTER TWENTY-ONE

Bélizon, behind his closed eyelids, is struggling to distance himself from the agony that threatens to swamp his senses. In his mind he tries to travel home to the cool water gardens of his presidential palace. He tries to retreat mentally to a time when he was young and vigorous and free of pain. But there is no escape. He opens his eyes once more and his gaze lights upon Edward Arden's perspiring face.

'Mr Arden,' he calls out, abruptly rapping with his knife on the little silver chalice, 'would you care to propose a toast to our French hosts?'

'Most certainly,' Arden croaks, rising unsteadily to his feet. 'I should be honoured and delighted. Nay, *delighted* so to do.' He picks up his empty wineglass and looks at it in bemusement until Van der Pump, standing stiffly behind the President's chair, calls out to one of the waitresses,

'For Christ's sake give the man some more wine or we shall be here until sunup.' Arden waits glumly for his glass to be filled before mumbling,

'To our hosts.'

'No, no, no, Mr Arden,' Bélizon chides. 'That really won't do. Won't do at all. Allow me to prompt you. Repeat after me, "To our gracious Gallic hosts,"' and Arden meekly repeats the words. '"To French savoir-faire,"' Bélizon persists, '"to French generosity and last, but by no means least, to French cuisine."' Arden stumbles through the short speech and slumps back heavily into his seat. 'Well said,' Bélizon remarks with a brief chuckle, before addressing the whole table once more.

'The English, you will find, have something of an inferiority complex when it comes to their Gallic confrères, and is it to be wondered at? After all, the French have style, the French have chic, the French have Yves Saint-Laurent. The English have Marks & Spencer. The French have *haute cuisine*, the English have Pot Noodles. The French have sex, the English have Horlicks. I trust you are translating all this for your companions, Mr Arden.' Arden, squirming with discomfiture, manages to convey the gist of the speech to the dignitaries on either side of him, much to their merriment. Still Bélizon does not relinquish his grip.

'The French believe in strong government, in leadership. They are not swayed by world opinion. The French would never have treated poor General Pinochet in such a dishonourable manner.' Bélizon is gratified by the nods of assent from members of the French contingent.

He winces once more as the pain takes hold and Hortense rests a hand on his sleeve, studying him with curiosity rather than concern.

'You not feelin' too good, Massa President?'

'Purgatory,' he hisses back, 'sheer bloody purgatory, my dear. But it will pass. One way or another, it will pass.' He reaches into the top pocket of his uniform and takes out a small silver pillbox. 'One of these fellows should do the trick.' She watches as he swallows a large yellow capsule and the company resumes its several muted conversations.

At the opposite end of the table, Arden continues to drink, the wine fuelling his new-found courage and patriotic indignation. He rises unsteadily to his feet once more and announces, 'I wish to tell a joke.' Another uncomfortable silence descends as Arden, swaying back on his heels, continues. 'Actually, it's more of a riddle than a joke. Are you ready? Well then, here goes: "What's the difference between the French and a piece of toast?" Eh? What's the difference? Don't you know?' He peers blearily down at the sea of embarrassed faces gazing expectantly back at him. 'Come on. Jack, you must know this one.' But Devenish looks away. 'All right, then, I'll tell you. The difference between the French and a piece

171

of toast is that you can make soldiers out of a piece of toast. Pretty good, eh? Perhaps, Mr President, you'd be so good as to translate.' But the babble of disconcerted voices which breaks out is swiftly interrupted by the unexpected appearance of Polly. The child stands yawning on the threshold to the veranda, barefoot in her wispy cotton shift, dangling Arden's doll from one hand and knuckling her eyes with the other.

Diana starts to rise, but Ted anticipates her, pushing back his chair and joining Polly in the doorway. 'No, no, Diana. Please allow me,' he insists, taking the child's hand. 'Do not curtail the pleasures of the evening. I will take Polly back to her room and settle her down again. Apart from anything else, I feel in need of a breath of fresh air.' Diana studies the pair of them for a moment and nods. Arden makes a courteous, if clumsy, bow in the direction of Bélizon and leads Polly out across the decking into the darkness of the garden beyond.

CHAPTER TWENTY-TWO

Well, bugger me. I mean, who'd have thought it of old Ted? You had to hand it to him. It was an old joke, of course, but more power to him for standing up and stuffing it to the French like that. Went right over most of their heads, as usual, but it cheered the rest of us up no end. Even that old vulture Bélizon couldn't keep a straight face. I thought Diana looked a bit dubious about letting Ted put the little moppet back to bed, and as it turned out she was probably right to worry – but I'm getting ahead of myself again.

We polished off the chicken, washing it down, I'm bound to report, with a thunderingly good Burgundy, and then came the cheeses. After a sorbet that tasted to me like pomegranate, laced with marc, Magali came in to take a bow, followed by Gaston, pushing a candlelit trolley creaking with individual portions of the notorious *Baba au Rhum de la Maison*. Magali had once confided to me that she'd purloined the recipe from some fancy hotel restaurant in Monte Carlo. It was pretty much your standard rum baba, except that you got to choose the particular bottle of rum which took your fancy.

Bélizon got first shout, of course, and Gaston steered him in the direction of a dark and ancient demerara, which I happened to know was 151° proof spirit. Magali sloshed it on, lathered the whole thing in *crème Chantilly* and set it down in front of the old bastard. He sniffed at it, then raised his chalice to her, smiled and said,

'Madame, you are an artist. I thank you most sincerely for your hospitality tonight and I compliment you warmly on your sublime skill. I call upon those present to drink a toast,

'To Madame Delacroix and *la haute cuisine*.'

We all staggered to our feet again and duly drank the toast, although the old boy didn't even try to stand up. Magali stood there, struggling without much success to put a smile on her face. Gaston tried to make up for it by standing beside her with his arm round her shoulders, beaming and bowing at the assembled company like one of those little dipping birds you get in the souvenir shops. I must confess that I was feeling distinctly woozy from that point on in the proceedings, and the rest of the company managed to achieve varying levels of inebriation. One of Bélizon's mob actually passed out face down in the ruins of his rum baba, and a couple of Guitry's boys were trying to start up a glee club down at their end of the table, singing what I took to be dirty French rugby songs.

In the midst of all this drunken revelry Bélizon, having taken hardly one mouthful of his pud, let out an abrupt little yelp and his face crumpled up with pain. He clapped his hand to his side and made an unsuccessful attempt to get up, but he only succeeded in lolling sideways across the arm of his chair until one of his goons – might even have been Winston – stepped smartly forward and lifted him bodily out of his seat, cradling him gently in his arms like a sickly babe. Van der Pump frowned and looked at his watch. The old boy waved one of his knobbly claws feebly towards Hortense and croaked,

'Please, come with me. Come upstairs with me and be my nurse. You must come with me. I can't trust any of them. You must come and take care of me, mop my fevered brow. Keep me safe from harm . . .' Hortense tossed her napkin in my lap as Van der Pump took her elbow and led her off in the old boy's wake.

The rest of us just sort of sat there, belching and farting and twiddling our thumbs. One or two of us made a valiant stab at finishing off our rum babas, but most of the company were that far gone, it was strictly 'nil by mouth'. Coffee came round, I seem to remember, and there may have been a decanter of port. I'm almost certain there was a bottle of Calvados involved at one point. You have to appreciate that my account of events from here on in may be a little hazy, but I'm pretty sure I can give you the general nub of the gist.

CHAPTER TWENTY-THREE

Upstairs the bodyguard lays his fragile burden on the ancient creaking bed in Bélizon's room and with an unexpected and fastidious gentleness, removes the presidential boots. Hortense stands just inside the door, unsure of what is expected of her. She is confused by her feelings towards the old man. She feels as repelled as ever by the history of his infamy, by the knowledge of harm done to her and her kinfolk in the old country. But at the same time she feels forced into a reluctant and uncomfortable alliance with him in this situation through the shared colour of their skin. His pain disturbs her. Watching his anguish she cannot simply laugh it off and say to herself, as she would have done only a week before – 'Let him suffer – serve the evil bastard right.'

The guard unfastens the buttons of Bélizon's uniform and the old man pants and grimaces with the struggle of freeing himself from the closely tailored tunic. With a final determined effort he shrugs himself free of the broad maroon braces and lies back on the pillows.

'Come over here and sit by me,' he whispers at last, beckoning Hortense with one trembling brown finger. She tiptoes across the room and perches on the edge of a bedside chair. Bélizon dismisses the guard with a feeble wave of the hand. 'Wait outside. This young lady will do me no injury.'

When the door has closed, Hortense asks,

'What make you so sure of that, Massa President? What make you so goddamn cocky sure I won't put one of these pillows over your face and send you all to hell and gone?'

'You'd rather watch me suffer.'

'Now, ain't that the truth and no mistake.'

'You believe in hell?'

'Shit, no. Only hell I can see is the one that wicked old fuckers like you make for us right down here.'

'It is a point of view.'

'So what for you bring me up here?' she asks briskly, leaning over him to rearrange the pillows. 'You want I should do some nasty stuff to that sad old body of yours? You want maybe a quick hand job? Cost ya bob or two.'

'Ah, but wouldn't that be a fine thing, if it were possible? But I am afraid that nothing down there works much any more.'

'That right? Too bad. I had a uncle like that once.'

'In fact,' he adds, once again closing his eyes and letting his head loll back against the carved pine headboard, 'nothing much works up here, either.'

'So what the hell am I goin' do for you then? How am I goin' entertain you? I can't sing. But I can dance some – just like they once say 'bout that Fred Astaire.'

'Do you see, do you see over there on the table? Do you see a leather satchel? Would you be so good as to bring it to me?'

She saunters across the room and picks up the bag. It feels empty. As she hands it to him she says,

'Sho's hell ain't filled with no gold bullion.'

'Good as,' he grunts. He unbuckles the twin straps and, clutching the satchel to his chest so that she cannot see inside, thrusts his hand into one of its front pockets and with a conjuror's flourish produces a small square glassine envelope. He places it in her hand and says, 'A small token of my esteem, young lady.'

Hortense pokes the envelope beneath the shade of a standard lamp and studies it against the light in some bewilderment. Through the semi-transparent paper she can make out four coloured shapes, a triangle and three rectangles.

'Stamps?' she says, uncertainly. 'You think maybe I should get meself a hobby, like? Start a stamp collection?'

'That is all the collection you will need, my dear, believe

me. Those four stamps are worth 50,000 US dollars to any dealer, anywhere in the world. Finest currency known to man, and supremely portable. You can carry millions around in your back pocket and nobody is any the wiser.'

'And you want me to have this?' she asks, goggling, slack-mouthed at the prospect. He nods, and she adds, frowning suspiciously, 'So what I got to do for that sort of money?'

'Just take your clothes off and let me look at your body for a while.'

'That it?' she asks, warily, tucking the envelope away in her evening pouch.

'And talk to me, until I fall asleep.'

'You got it,' she exclaims, wriggling out of her dress. 'You want me to strut about some, show you all the goodies? You want I should play with meself a bit?'

He shakes his head, his glittering eyes fixed on the frizzy wedge of her pubic hair.

'No, just pull that armchair up closer to the bed and sit yourself down.'

'Sure certain thing, boss,' she says, heaving the heavy chair into the lamplight and draping herself nonchalantly across it. 'They yo' stamps.' There is a long silence while he studies her and eventually she says, 'So what you want talk about?'

'What do they say about me these days? What do they say about me on this side of the border?'

'People say all kinds of stuff,' she tells him with a shrug. 'They say you starve your own people and keep all the aid money for yourself in Switzerland, or some such place. They say you have people arrested and tortured for no reason. They say anyone speak out against you get himself disappeared. They say you maybe should be locked up in some deep dark hole till yo' flesh rots off yo' bones. In short, the general view seems to be, Mr President, without intendin' any undue disrespect, that you are just about the evilest old buzzard ever lived.'

'And you agree with the general view?'

'Shit, I only just met you.'

'Evil? Is that the expression they use?'

'You reckon you not evil?'

'I don't begin to understand the concept. What is evil? I merely do what every creature does. I do what I must in order to survive.'

'Way I hear it, you do a whole heap of shit to make sure lots of other people *don't* survive.'

'That's the law of nature. We are but beasts and the weak must always be sacrificed in the interests of the strong. Tyranny is the only defensible form of government. Do you

181

know, the word "tyrant" was not always a pejorative term? In the ancient world a tyrant was merely someone who took charge, someone to be admired and respected. A strong leader who could provide stability for his people. With a tyrant, you knew where you were.'

'And in the end we all dead, anyhow.'

'Yes. In the end we are all dead.' His face reflects a fresh surge of pain.

'You scared of dyin'?' she asks quietly. He pauses before replying, seemingly in some kind of reverie,

'Let me tell you how my great-grandfather died. He was a plantation worker in Alabama and one fine day, at the age of twenty-six, he was accused completely out of the blue by one of the white women in the town of behaving in an over-familiar manner towards her. Note that I say, "accused" – there were no witnesses, no evidence of any kind. No suggestion that he'd laid so much as a finger on her. But she happened to be the daughter of the local mayor and that was all it took.

'That same night a party of vigilantes took him into the forest, where they blinded him with a hot iron, and ruptured both of his eardrums with meat skewers. Then they stripped him naked and hung him by his wrists from the branch of a tree. Over the next three days, they flogged him with split canes and bullwhips – not continuously, but at unpredictable intervals. He could not hear or see them coming. All he knew for that brief remainder of his life – although to him it must have seemed an eternity – was the sudden agony of the unexpected lash.'

'Jesus!' Hortense exclaims, craning forward now in her armchair, arms wrapped protectively about her. 'That the most wickedest thing I ever did hear tell about.'

'He lost his mind after the first few hours and dangled there, gibbering until he finally died of thirst. And do you know something? These men were not some crazed, drunken army on the rampage; they were ordinary farmers and shopkeepers. They were, in short, decent, God-fearing, white Americans.' Breathing heavily he stops to wipe an unexpected eruption of perspiration from his brow with brown, arthritic knuckles.

'Who would not fear dying in such a manner?' he resumes quietly. 'I fear pain, like all men. That is why torture is such a useful tool of the state. But I do not fear death. Death is nothing.'

'You reckon as how ain't nothing goin' survive?'

'Everything survives.'

'How you make that out?'

'Every particle of each one of us will survive our deaths. It's simply a matter of rearrangement. Ashes to ashes.'

'How come you quote so much from the Good Book?' she asks.

'The words of Jesus Christ are powerful magic for a tyrant. Persuade a man that he will be happy in the next world and he will put up with a great deal of misery in this one. Persuade him that his evil deeds will be punished by everlasting torment after death, and you can count on his good behaviour while he is alive. But take away the promise of heaven and the fear of hell and men will get up to all kinds of mischief.'

'Like you done, you mean?'

'When I die, do you know what I should like?' he continues dreamily, not hearing her question. 'I should like a memorial ceremony like the one Alexander the Great arranged for his mother. He was very fond of his mother, you know. Quite heartbroken when she died. So he had a vast funeral pyre built for her. It was in several layers, like a wedding cake, and he had singers imprisoned in each layer, according to the style of their voices. He had basses at the bottom, then baritones and so on, all the way up to boy trebles right at the top. When the torches were put to the thing, the screams of those trapped inside soared higher and higher in pitch as the flames crept up the structure. Just think what a magnificent spectacle that would have been to behold.'

Hortense sits watching him, an expression of bemused horror on her face.

'Shame you wouldn't be there to enjoy it,' she says at last.

'Oh, I very much doubt if anyone could engineer such an event in this day and age. There's bound to be some footling regulation against it. Some public health ordinance, I shouldn't wonder. Still and all, I must confess, you are a fine figure of a woman.'

CHAPTER TWENTY-FOUR

Somehow, we all seemed to end up on the veranda, with the French contingent crooning weepy sentimental ballads to one another and Bélizon's cronies raiding the humidor for the biggest stogies they could lay their sweaty paws on. Van der Pump returned to the party, muttering something about the old boy needing a good night's sleep. Diana and Guitry had installed themselves at a table by the front rail and the oily little clerk pulled out his watch with an expression of exasperation and said,

'Still half an hour until *les feux d'artifice*, and the man has retired to his bed. *Quel désastre.*'

'You don't think he's been poisoned, do you?' I asked him.

'*Hélas, non,*' he said with a small sigh. 'I think he has just consumed more alcohol than is prudent for a man in his delicate state of health. Well, I'm damned if I will miss these fireworks. This display is costing the French government more than 50,000 francs and I, for one, just adore fireworks.'

'Quite,' I agreed. 'Well, who doesn't?'

I fired up a Montecristo and struck out across the lawn towards the annexe, leaving the pair of them to their cosy tête-à-tête. I'm bound to confess that I was beginning to feel pretty cheesed off with the way things were working out. What with Hortense upstairs in *my* bedroom in *my* four-hundred-dollar frock, holding the hand of some psychopathic dictator, and Diana being dribbled over by a slippery little French bureaucrat, it seemed to me that I'd pretty much got the furry end of the lollipop that evening.

As I walked away from the veranda, the clamour of drunken revelry faded behind me, but I became aware of another sound. There was a noise, a creepy sort of wheezing and barking coming from the bushes near the little bungalow. I thought at first it must have been some sort of animal, a tapir perhaps, or one of the feral dogs that roamed the hills. I stepped gingerly across the grass and found Ted standing in one of the flowerbeds, no jacket or tie, his shirt-tails hanging out in the moonlight, bent double and retching like a cat with a terminal furball.

'Steady on, old son,' I said to him, relieved not to be confronting some rabid, slavering cur, 'take it easy now, deep breaths. If you've got to bring it up, just let it come. Better out than in is my advice – don't fight it.' My first assumption, you see, was that the combination of Gaston's lethal cocktails and

188

the high-octane rum babas had finally taken its toll. Then he looked at me and I have never seen such an expression of utter horror and confusion on the face of any man. His eyes were wide, red-rimmed and overflowing, the corners of his open mouth were pulled down into a macabre black hieroglyph of anguish. He stood there, swaying from side to side with his hands thrust down into his crotch, and he said,

'Vile, vile, vile. Christ forgive me for the vile thing I have done.'

'What are you on about?' I asked him, putting an arm round his shoulders. But he shook me off with a sort of shudder and went on,

'The child, the child. I have done such vile things, such foul, disgusting, *wicked* things. And to Polly. To that dear, sweet, innocent child.'

'My God, man,' I said, beginning to get a nasty feeling about the whole situation, 'what have you done to the child? You've not harmed her in some way, have you? Not hurt her?' He grabbed both my hands in his, painfully crushing the fingers in his wild grief and hissed into my face,

'Harmed her? I wish I'd killed her, I truly do. It would be better for her if she were dead. Then she would never remember, then she would never know – nobody would – the vile things that I have done.'

189

'Are you trying to tell me,' I asked him, the revulsion rising in my gorge, 'that you have been having some sort of perverted sex with the little piccaninny? You've been interfering with her?'

'I'm not sure what I've done,' was all he said. So I hit him, and I'm not ashamed to confess it. Hit him hard, a right hook, and he toppled slowly sideways into the bushes like a felled sapling. I looked down at his crumpled, whimpering face and I said,

'You filthy degenerate bastard pervert. I hope they lock you up and cut your willy off. I've a good mind to do it myself, here and now with this cigar cutter.' And I got it out and waved it in front of his eyes. But he wasn't seeing it. Wasn't seeing anything. I left him snivelling in the dirt.

Back at the veranda, I found Diana still making small talk with Guitry, so I just barged right in and told her,

'You'd best be getting back to your "charming young protégée". I believe something nasty may have happened to her – something involving Ted, I'm afraid. I think you'll find her in a bit of a state. You may want me to call a doctor.' And do you know, she frowned a bit, looked up at me with a face as calm as a millpond and then just nodded, for all the world as if she'd been expecting something of the kind.

CHAPTER TWENTY-FIVE

Arden lies very still, cradled by soft soil, the smell of damp humus in his nostrils and the babble of faraway conversation in his ears. He is aware that Devenish struck him, but he feels no pain. All he feels is a deeply bewildering self-disgust. The images that float unbidden before his inner eye trigger another bout of retching and he rolls over onto all fours, vomit erupting like a hot geyser from his stomach, leaving his throat raw and his teeth etched by acid bile. He has no idea of how much time passes, but eventually he rises unsteadily to his feet, aware now of a dull throbbing pain in his left cheekbone. Keeping to the shadows he makes for the villa, unsure of what he seeks, but knowing that he must find some balm for his tortured soul.

In the kitchen he finds only the sleeping Gaston, snoring loudly on a chair in front of the cellar door. Like a man wading waist-deep through a swamp, he crosses to the table where he sees a half-full bottle of rum and a wet glass. He sits down, pours himself a drink and stares dully about him at surroundings which are familiar, yet mysteriously uncomforting. Everything is as it always was, but there is something subtly different about every single item in the room. As the rum rolls warmly down his gullet, he suffers the dawning realization that it is he who has forever changed. He sees that by his vile actions he has transformed himself out of all recognition from the decent man he knew himself to be two hours before. He has become a monster. A child molester. A pervert. He has cast himself beyond the pale.

He contemplates with rising panic and despair the future which must lie in wait for him; arrest and interrogation, arbitrary beatings by the police to register their righteous disgust at his offence, a trial, public humiliation and then what? Some French jail, where he will be the target of unremitting attacks from fellow inmates, no less disgusted by his loathsome crime than he himself. He would not survive a week, he suspects, under such conditions. He helps himself to another two fingers of rum but when he attempts to cap the bottle, the cork evades his nerveless fingers and bounces across the floor. He stoops to retrieve it and his eye lights on the Desert Eagle resting beneath Gaston's chair. Now he senses what has to happen next. Now he knows that he must do the decent thing. He staggers when he bends to pick up the gun, startled by its obstinate weight, but Gaston does not stir.

Up in his moonlit bedroom, Arden examines the weapon. The model is unfamiliar to him but, prompted by some dim recollection of his officer training, he checks the action and the magazine and manages to identify the ambidextrous safety catches to either side of the hammer. He sits quietly on the edge of his bed for a time, gazing blankly through the open windows at the silvered profile of far mountains and fancies he hears the distant trickle of water into a cool, green rock pool. He takes the gun in his right hand and raises it to his temple, but the position is an awkward one, because of the length of the barrel, and he fears that the angle may not be right for a clean kill. He is surprised to note, with the suddenly acquired dispassion of an outsider, that his hand has stopped trembling. But even as he readies himself for whatever awaits him in the afterlife, a part of him cannot help imagining the mess he is about to make in his room, a room which he has always proudly maintained in a state of scrupulous tidiness. Light-headed at the absurdity of this foible, he nonetheless stands up and walks slowly out onto the balcony, where he turns his back on the mountains, raises the gun once more and tentatively pushes the end of the long barrel into his open mouth.

What does he feel? Not fear, surprisingly, but a kind of foolish self-consciousness, as though he is doing all this for the benefit of some unseen audience. He wonders if this is normal. What do suicides usually feel before they commit that final, irrevocable act? We can never know. When will he do it? Will he count to three and pull the trigger? Or maybe ten. Or will counting to ten take too long and weaken his resolve? Already these thoughts have taken him longer than it would take to count to ten. Three it is, then, he decides.

At his count of two there is a deafening concussive report, and a blinding flash of light from outside silhouettes him in the mirror of his open wardrobe door. He stands, motionless, examining the internal after-image of his outlined shape, and struggling to comprehend how he can have fired early and yet survived. As he lowers the gun, there are more explosions and in the mirror the darkness behind him blossoms into a shimmering chrysanthemum of golden light. He turns to see the whole sky cupped in twinkling, tumbling trails like the ribs inside a luminous parasol. The fireworks have finally begun.

He begins to laugh, and as he turns to stand at the balcony rail, watching the show through tear-filled eyes, he cannot help but wonder what kind of man could kill himself before the end of a firework display? Below him, from the veranda, he can hear the exaggerated exclamations of euphoria from the drunken delegates as each new burst of light and noise pummels its way down from the skies. Then in one of the sudden silences between explosions, he hears a noise to his left, the creak of an opening door. Alphonse Bélizon, in a pale singlet and uniform trousers held up by broad scarlet braces, staggers forth to stand on his own balcony and enjoy the presidential fireworks. Although the light spilling from the room behind the slight, trembling figure leaves his face in darkness, Arden fancies he can see a smile on the man's lips. As the celestial barrage resumes with renewed violence, Arden raises the gun, holding it steady with both hands, as he has been trained to do, and whispers under his breath,

'Becky.'

He fires once. The bullet, which takes the President under the right arm, is deflected to the rear by a rib, shattering the fourth thoracic vertebra and the left scapula before exiting, through a wound the size of a fist, to lose itself in the indifferent night. Arden is hurled back by the recoil and lies crumpled and breathless against his balcony rails. As the fireworks reach the crescendo of their meaningless celebration of light and noise, Bélizon's already lifeless body, itself flung sideways by the impact, topples over the balcony rail and falls through the roof of the veranda beneath. After a moment, the naked Hortense steps out through the open doorway, surveys the scene and, hearing a sound, turns to look at Arden as he struggles to his feet, still clutching the gun. The final triumphant panoply of magnesium fire invests both of their faces with a ghostly blue pallor.

'My, my, Mr Arden,' she says to him, in the sudden silence, 'I do believe you done shot yourself a president.'

CHAPTER TWENTY-SIX

My God, you never saw the like of it, well, I never did at any rate. Just as the fireworks were building up to the grand finale, there was this crash behind us like the fall of Jericho and when we looked round, there was Bélizon lying all crumpled up on the trestle table, spread-eagled among the shattered remnants of punchbowls, glasses and slats from the veranda roof, his blood-red eyeballs like a pair of maraschino cherries staring wide and bright. Pandemonium then, of course, everyone rushing about in all directions shouting and trying to see what had happened. I looked up through the hole in the roof and into the face of one of the goons looking back down from the balcony. Winston, who was standing near me, went a sort of dull ochre colour and started jabbering like a maniac. Mind you, I suppose the poor sod was even more put out than the rest of us, what with him being part of the President's personal bodyguard and one thing and another. Naturally, I was gawking away with the rest of them, but I'm bound to report that there was something distinctly fishy about Van der Pump's behaviour. The moment he'd registered that his guv'nor had dropped out of the sky, he stepped down from the lighted veranda onto the lawn and stood with his hands on his hips, staring up into the darkness of the hills. Then he looked at his watch, held it up to his ear and shook it. Now what, I ask you, was that all about?

Hortense suddenly materialized beside me, looking a touch dishevelled I thought, and I asked her,

'D'you know what happened?'

'Fell off the balcony is all I see. Went outside to take in the fireworks and took a dive over the balustrade. I figure he must have had some kind of stroke or heart attack or somethin'.' But then I heard Guitry's squeaky little voice call out,

'This man has been shot. There is a wound here, see. And here, where the bullet escaped again.' Van der Pump returned to the scene at that moment and parted the throng around the body. He looked it up and down like it was a piece of second-hand furniture that wasn't entirely to his taste, then turned to Guitry and said,

'Where's the American? Where's Horowitz?' Guitry looked blank and did one of his Gallic shrugs.

'I have no idea. He was not at the dinner. Who knows where he might be. Is it important, do you think?' Guitry seemed to be having trouble believing his ears.

198

'I saw him earlier,' I volunteered. 'He was all lathered up because he thought his room had been turned over.'

'Jesus Christ,' Van der Pump said quietly. 'He'll be long gone, you bet your life. The chubby little bastard'll be well on his way back to the Blue Ridge Mountains of Virginia by now, you take it from me.'

'You think he did this?' I asked, trying to keep the disbelief out of my voice.

'Not personally. But he sure as hell arranged the hit, and you'd better believe it. Shit, I should have seen this coming.'

'So who did fire the shot?' Guitry asked, looking increasingly like a man who'd strayed into a madhouse and wasn't sure which of those present were members of staff.

'Professional. Somewhere up in the hills back there. Don't worry, we'll get him. There's only one way down. I want the body taken inside and laid out. Nobody is to touch it after that – do I make myself clear? I will arrange for the remains to be flown home first thing tomorrow morning.'

'But of course,' Guitry said, spreading his palms wide, 'you must make whatever arrangements you consider proper under the circumstances.'

All of which I found a bit bloody odd, to tell you the truth. I mean, normally, you get a case of sudden death – even some anonymous vagrant, and in no time at all, you're up to your armpits in detectives and photographers and pathologists in white paper suits. Stripy tape all over the shop, nobody touches anything, nobody leaves the scene until they've given a statement and even after that it's weeks before everything gets properly sorted out. Here we had the assassination of a head of state on foreign soil and they were carting him off the premises like a bundle of soiled hotel bedlinen. As I watched Winston and one of the other goons carry the body inside, it occurred to me that there was a bit more to this than met the eye.

CHAPTER TWENTY-SEVEN

'Go back inside,' Hortense tells Arden, as she ducks back through the lighted doorway. She scrambles into her dress, crosses swiftly to the door and tells the dozing body-guard in the corridor outside that there has been an accident. He barges past her and runs through to look over the balcony. She hurries along to Arden's room where she relieves him of the gun, and leads him by the hand down the dimly lit service stairs to the hotel linen room. Beneath the pallid glare of the single fluorescent tube she wipes the weapon carefully with a soiled table napkin before wrapping it and tucking it away at the bottom of one of the wicker hampers.

It will be found three days later by the local laundry and the police will make investigations at the hotel. But without a spent bullet on which to perform comparative ballistic testing, they will be unable to identify it as the assassination weapon. After two days of probing, they will be instructed from the highest level to drop the case. Gaston will deny all knowledge of the weapon and will remain forever convinced that one of the bodyguards, most probably Winston, stole the gun, but since it was never legally his, he cannot press the point and must console himself with moaning to Magali for years to come about the loss of his most prized possession.

At Hortense's urging, Arden returns to his room while she makes her way back to the party on the veranda. For two hours, he sits on the edge of his bed, listening uncomprehendingly to the distant ebb and flow of events unfolding beneath him. He is a man borne irresistibly forward on the breaking edge of the wave of history, which, as always, is compounded from countless minor casual accidents. A lost child rescued. A fishing boat found abandoned. An automatic pistol stolen from a drunken Belgian. A glass of aquavit. The abduction of a Jewish translator. The diseased kidney of a petty despot. Fireworks. He feels like a man cut loose from the world, like in a dream of flying. He has no fear of the drop, finding only exhilaration in his weightlessness, his detachment from reality. He stretches out on the bed, ankles crossed and palms together on his chest like a stone crusader on a tomb, and he sleeps.

CHAPTER TWENTY-EIGHT

Late the following morning, nursing an apocalyptic hangover, I was perched on the veranda steps trying to discover the least painful angle at which to lean my throbbing head against the woodwork. Van der Pump flopped down gleefully beside me, slapped me on the thigh with one of those slabby mitts of his and exclaimed,

'We only got the bastard, didn't we? Cornered him up in the rocks just after sun up. Tried to shoot his way out, like the stupid arsehole he was, and so we were forced to open fire. Put twenty-six slugs in him. Hell of a mess.'

'How do you know it was him?'

'No question. He had the gun with the night 'scope, photographs of the President, the works. His position gave him a clear line of sight over the back of the hotel. Couldn't miss.' He laid his hand on my leg again and squeezed in what I suppose he thought was a friendly manner. Felt like being bitten by an alligator. I looked down at his fingers and there on the little one was this socking great gold ring with an emerald in it. An emerald as big as an olive. 'And d'you know the funny thing, Jacko?' he went on. 'It was the guy you'd warned me about. The guy who'd been waving his money around all over town. We found more than seven thousand US dollars in his rucksack. Well-known contract killer, name of Vargas. Brazilian. Bit past his prime, mind you. Bit running to seed, you might say. Fucking alcoholic, not to put too fine a point on it.'

'So that's that, then?'

'Sure thing. We're flying the body out even as we speak and Alphonse Junior will be duly sworn in this afternoon as the second president of the republic.'

'Foregone conclusion, is it?'

'Best thing for the country, in my view. Sure, there'll be some changes made, but I think you could confidently say we've got the right man for the job.'

'Any news of Horowitz?'

'Naah. Didn't expect any, neither. We searched his room last night. Found a whole load of dollars with serial numbers close to the roll we took off Vargas. Sloppy work, really, for Langley.'

'Gaston had some notion that the idiot boy was working for American intelligence.'

'No doubt about it. Uncle Sam caught in the act once more,

dabbling his grubby fingers in the clear blue waters of the Caribbean.'

'Well,' I was struggling for something useful to say, 'quick work, then. Job well done.'

'You'd better believe it,' he said, fixing me once more with those little rabbit eyes. And you know, he didn't say it like you normally would – like Hortense would say it – sort of off the cuff. He said it as though he really meant it. That I was to believe it, or something mighty unpleasant would happen to me. 'One last thing,' he went on. 'You don't happen to know where your partner in crime was last night when the President was shot?'

'Who do you mean, Ted?'

'Yes, Ted. Where was he?'

'Out in the garden somewhere. We'd had a bit of an argy-bargy and I'd thumped him, I'm afraid. Left him curled up in one of the flowerbeds over there.' He looked out across the lawn to where I was pointing and then squinted up through the hole in the roof.

'Fair enough,' he said.

When he'd wandered off inside, I lit up a cheroot and set off to take a stroll round the grounds. Almost at once I spotted Diana coming across from the annexe.

'How is she?' I called out to her.

'Polly?' she answered airily, striding up to me. 'She's fine. Whatever gave you the idea that something had happened to her?' Sort of took the wind out of my sails a bit, that, as you can well imagine.

'You mean nothing *has* happened to her?'

'Not so far as I can tell. When I went over last night, she was sound asleep in her bed. Did you say that Ted was somehow involved?'

'Must have got the wrong end of the stick, I suppose. Misunderstanding. Well, glad the little lady's all right.' Bewildered was not the word for it. I was flabbergasted. I mean, I know I'd had a skinful, but surely I couldn't have missed Ted's drift to that extent. Maybe I had got it all arse about face. Or perhaps he'd imagined the whole thing, being pissed as a poodle, like the rest of us. But then I thought, you wouldn't even *imagine* a thing like that, would you? However arseholed you got, you wouldn't get fantasies about interfering with kiddies, would you, unless you were a real dyed-in-the-wool degenerate.

Ted showed up at breakfast sporting a plum-coloured shiner and sat down at his usual table without saying a dickybird. And that was pretty much the end of our friendship. We exchanged frosty pleasantries for a time, whenever the occasion demanded. Then a couple of weeks later he packed his bags and went back to England. Last I heard, his mail was being forwarded to an address in Eastbourne or somewhere. Looking back, he was always rather a sad little bastard. One of those men who passes through life having absolutely no effect on anything. When he dies, it'll be as though he'd never been born.

I stayed on at the Auberge and after the first week or so when the place was overrun with reporters and television crews things returned pretty much to normal. Hortense went a bit strange. Packed in her old trade – which was a loss – and opened a frock shop down on the esplanade. God knows who bankrolled her – some local gangster, I shouldn't wonder, although Gaston told me she was passing on all the profits to Diana's Polly fund.

When the story got round about the assassination, the hotel became notorious for a time. There were even a few package tours laid on from Europe – gawping tossers in nylon sports shirts and plastic sandals, paying through the nose to sleep in the room where Alphonse Bélizon snuffed it. Kept me in firewater, though, telling them the story in the bar every night, just like I'm telling you. I simply gave it to them straight, mind you. I kept my suspicions to myself, like Van der Pump had recommended. I mean, it's a damn fine yarn as it stands, isn't it, without trying to turn it into some convoluted conspiracy theory?

CHAPTER TWENTY-NINE

Shortly after dawn, Van der Pump and Guitry climb the ridge above the hotel. Guitry, in shirtsleeves, his hair still unkempt and spiky, is breathing heavily as he struggles to keep up with the big South African.

'*Mon dieu.* So what happened?' he asks.

'Fucked if I know, exactly,' Van der Pump tells him. 'It sure as shit wasn't "plan A".'

'The French government will not be held responsible for this, you realize.'

'The fucking French government was never going to be held responsible, if you recall. That was the whole point of shipping in *that* bunch of deadbeats.' He gestures with a sweep of his arm to the troops breaking camp lower down the rise.

'Did Vargas really kill him?'

'Fat fucking chance. Vargas was so pissed he couldn't have stopped a pig in a passage. Besides which, he was already dead by the time the fireworks began.'

'*Merde, quelle bagarre!* And your own marksman, what of him?'

'Standing by. Waiting for the order.'

'So who *did* kill him?'

'Jesus only knows. Some genuine fucking terrorist, more than likely. The only two people not accounted for at the Auberge were the American and Mister Edward Arden.'

Down the hill, in the breakfast room, Arden keeps himself to himself, avoids eye contact, especially with Jack. He finishes his second cup of coffee and steps out on to the veranda where, before he can retreat, he comes face to face with Diana.

'Ted,' she says, taking his arm, 'I think we should have a little talk, don't you?' She leads him off across the lawn, and looking back over his shoulder he sees the sneering expression on Devenish's face.

'I believe I owe you something of an explanation,' she begins, 'perhaps even an apology. I have never been totally frank with you about Polly's background, and from what she tells me, something may have happened last night between the two of you which we must all find ... highly regrettable. You see, when I found Polly, she was working in a brothel.'

'My God.'

'She was sold to the . . . to the *establishment* concerned at the tender age of six.'

'You are saying she must have seen things, then? She must have seen revolting things, she must have been familiar with what goes on in those places.'

'Not just *seen*, Edward. She wasn't there to scrub floors and carry drinks. She was a prostitute. She was a child prostitute.'

'Oh, no. Oh, dear God, say it can't be true.'

'That is the only life she has ever really known. Her dealings with men have all been of the same kind. You could say that she knows of no other way to please them.'

'But that does not excuse what I did. Nothing can ever excuse the vile, vile thing that happened.'

'Nor can I pretend to offer you any consolation, even if I wanted to. But I did think you deserved to know the full story. I have always found morality a perplexing and elusive subject. I believe you are at heart a good, kind man.'

'But I cannot see how this absolves me,' Arden murmurs at last. 'I have acted as badly in this business as a man ever could. It is worse than anything I could imagine.'

'Worse even than murder?' she asks quietly. In response to his look of panic, she goes on, 'Hortense told me what you did last night – do not be alarmed, I'm not about to tell anyone else. But she and I have no secrets. What you did was magnificent. If it were ever to be known, there would be a square named after you in every democratic capital in the Caribbean. It was a heroic thing to do. Should you need – how shall I put it? – an alibi, I would be proud to swear that you spent the night with me.'

'I did it for Rebecca. It had nothing to do with anyone else, it was between him and me. And I do not believe that it was a good thing to do. I am ready to face the consequences of my actions.'

'Sometimes, Ted,' she says, linking her arm through his once more to walk him back, 'I believe that a bad act can also be a good deed.'

As Van der Pump and Guitry descend to the hotel, the Frenchman is still showing signs of nervous agitation.

'So, the American we are saying was CIA?' he asks.

'*Krikt*. That should keep the Yanks out of your back yard for a good ten years.'

'And *was* he?'

'Not a chance. He was just what he said he was; a dumb fucking tourist.'

'How can you be so sure?'

'We asked him.' Guitry looks sceptical. 'We asked him,' Van der Pump insists, 'very, *very* thoroughly.'

'Please, please,' Guitry says, throwing up his hands, 'this I do not need to know. So the money, the dollars in his room – this was your idea?'

'A little bit of improvisation on my part, I confess. Improvisation – life and soul of guerrilla warfare.'

Some days later, the body of Horowitz will be discovered up in the hills. In addition to the mutilation caused by feral dogs, there will be clear signs of torture. The pathologist will find evidence of more than two hundred cigarette burns on the remaining skin. Mute testimony both to the persistence of his interrogators and the depth of his ignorance. The US State Department will deny any connection between the dead student and the Central Intelligence Agency and will, on this occasion, be telling the truth.

'So what about Monsieur Arden?' Guitry persists. 'I do not see him as a terrorist.'

'Me neither. But I'll tell you one thing. From the state of the wound, assuming the old bastard was looking out at the fireworks, the shot was fired from his right side. It was nobody up close – there were no burns – so it couldn't have been the black hooker. But it could have been fired, say, from the balcony of Arden's room.'

'Do we need to investigate further?' the Frenchman persists, as they reach the veranda steps.

'Christ, no. But I will have a sociable chat with Mr Arden. In the unlikely event that it *was* him, we wouldn't want him doing something embarrassing like confessing, would we now?'

Arden has returned to his room to begin sorting through his clothes and his few other possessions. One thing he knows for certain. He cannot remain at the hotel. As he stares at the meaningless flotsam of his solitary life, he becomes aware of Van der Pump standing in the open doorway.

'I was expecting you,' the Englishman says.

'And why would that be, Mr Arden? Surely you have nothing to contribute to our investigation of last night's events? As I was telling your compatriot downstairs, we already know the man responsible.'

'Yes, well, I daresay it was only a matter of time.'

'Extremely dangerous international terrorist called Vargas. Tried to shoot his way past us. Didn't make it.' Arden takes a deep breath and hears the blood pounding in his ears. The air feels heavy, viscous.

'I see. Well, I suppose congratulations are . . .' He pauses in mid-sentence as the huge South African bends to pick up a small item from beside the skirting board. Van der Pump examines his find and tosses the spent cartridge case nonchalantly to Arden, saying, 'Place needs a bit of a tidy-up.

214

'Let me make something absolutely clear, Mr Arden,' the big albino continues. 'There is nothing – absolutely *nothing* anybody needs to know from you. Nothing anybody *wants* to know. But I do suggest you would perhaps be happier – or should I say *safer* – living somewhere other than on the island. You should count yourself a very lucky man. A very lucky man indeed.'

By the end of the week, Arden has made arrangements to move back to England where he will live out the remaining seventeen years of his life with his sister in a bungalow near Worthing. Because of his moustache, the local schoolchildren will chant 'I am the Walrus' when they pass his gate.